WE GODDESSES

A RICHARD JACKSON BOOK

WE GODDESSES

ATHENA · APHRODITE · HERA

BY DORIS ORGEL

ILLUSTRATED BY
MARILEE HEYER

A DK INK BOOK
DK PUBLISHING, INC.

A Richard Jackson Book

DK Publishing, Inc., 95 Madison Avenue, New York, New York 10016

Visit us on the World Wide Web at http://www.dk.com

Library of Congress Cataloging-in-Publication Data
Orgel, Doris.
We goddesses : Athena, Aphrodite, Hera / by Doris Orgel;
illustrated by Marilee Heyer.—1st ed.
p. cm.
"A DK Ink book."
Summary: Three Greek goddesses, Athena, Aphrodite, and Hera,
tell their own stories. Includes information about Greek society and religion.
ISBN 0-7894-2586-6
[1. Goddesses, Greek—Fiction. 2. Mythology, Greek—Fiction.
3. Greece—Fiction.] I. Heyer, Marilee, ill. II. Title.
PZ7.0632We 1999 [Fic]—dc21 98-41155 CIP AC

Book design by Jennifer Browne.
The illustrations for this book were created with watercolor, ink, and colored pencil.
The text of this book is set in 14 point Goudy Oldstyle.

Printed and bound in USA.
First Edition, 1999
2 4 6 8 10 9 7 5 3 1

For Jennifer Kemp

I want to thank Mark Benford, Rebecca Liebman-Smith,
Jamie Pittel, Hannah Tepper, and Sara Weiss for their thoughtful comments
and suggestions. I also want to thank my agent, Amy Berkower,
for helping me dream up this book. Last and most,
I'm grateful to Richard Jackson for his brilliant editing.

CONTENTS

   *(In which she tells how she burst from Zeus's head—but reveals
a deeper secret of her birth; tells of her childhood with Triton,
the river god who raised her; playing with his daughter, Pallas, her
dear friend; Pallas's death; how she, Athena, was welcomed on
Mount Olympus; her heroes; her defense of her virginity; Perseus
and Medusa; how Pegasus was born; how he released "the horse's*

spring," source of poets' inspiration; she tells of Poseidon, her rival; his pursuit of Demeter; his creating odd new animals: the zebra, camel, and giraffe; how she, Athena, competed with him to become the champion of Athens; how, and with whose help, she won; and how she wants to be remembered in millennia to come.)

Aphrodite   29
  (In which she tells of her birth from the sea; her journeys with Zephyrus to Cythera and Cyprus; her arrival on Olympus and adoption by Zeus, who gave her a husband, Hephaestus; troubles over lovers; the wedding of Thetis and King Peleus; Eris's "gift" of the golden apple; Myrrha, who turned into a myrrh tree as she gave birth to Adonis; Adonis killed by a boar; her love for Anchises; the birth of Aeneas; the judgment of Paris; Helen and King Menelaus; how Paris stole Helen away; how that started the war between Greece and Troy; how even gods and goddesses joined in the fighting; she tells of the wound that she suffered while protecting her dear son Aeneas; how the rainbow goddess Iris rescued her; and of the splendid city founded by Aeneas, and of her pride in him.)

Hera   61
  (In which she tells of being swallowed with her brothers and sisters by their father, Cronos; their mother, Rhea, setting them free; her encounter with Zeus; his courtship; his overthrowing Cronos and dividing up the world; his "previous marriages"; the world's first and most sacred wedding; Gaia's visitation gift: the golden apple tree; the wedding night, three hundred years long, yet all too brief; the question to Tiresias next morning: who, the bride or groom, has greater joy from love?; Tiresias's answer; her discovery that Zeus betrayed his marriage vows; she tells of Typhaon, her monster-son, born out of her despair;

LIST OF ILLUSTRATIONS

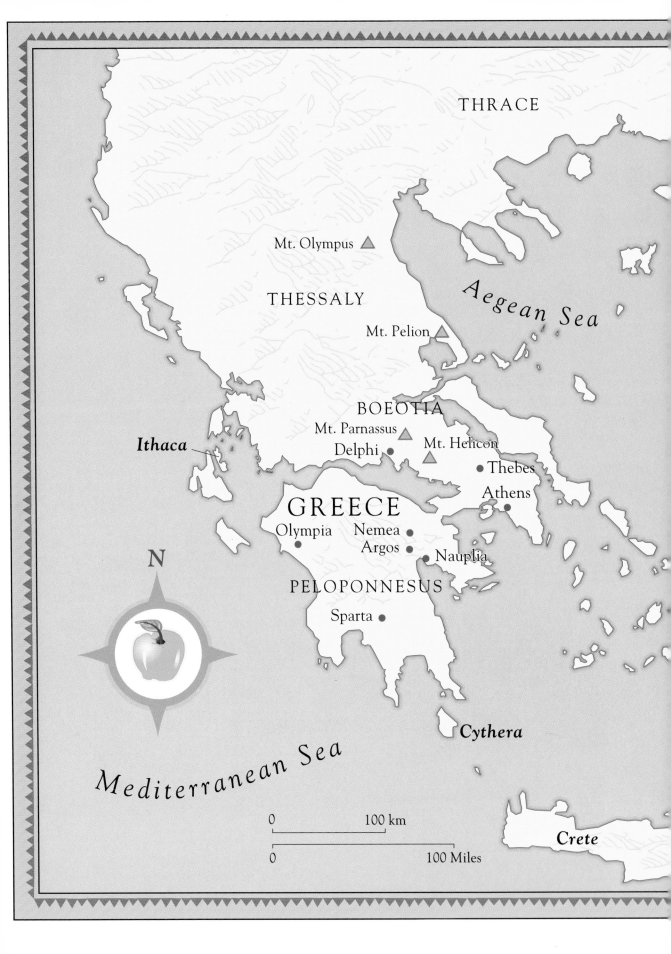

THRACE

Mt. Olympus △

THESSALY

Mt. Pelion △

Aegean Sea

BOEOTIA

Mt. Parnassus △

Ithaca

Delphi ●

Mt. Helicon △

● Thebes

Athens ●

GREECE

Olympia ●

Nemea ●

Argos ●

Nauplia ●

N

PELOPONNESUS

Sparta ●

Cythera

Mediterranean Sea

0	100 km
0	100 Miles

Crete

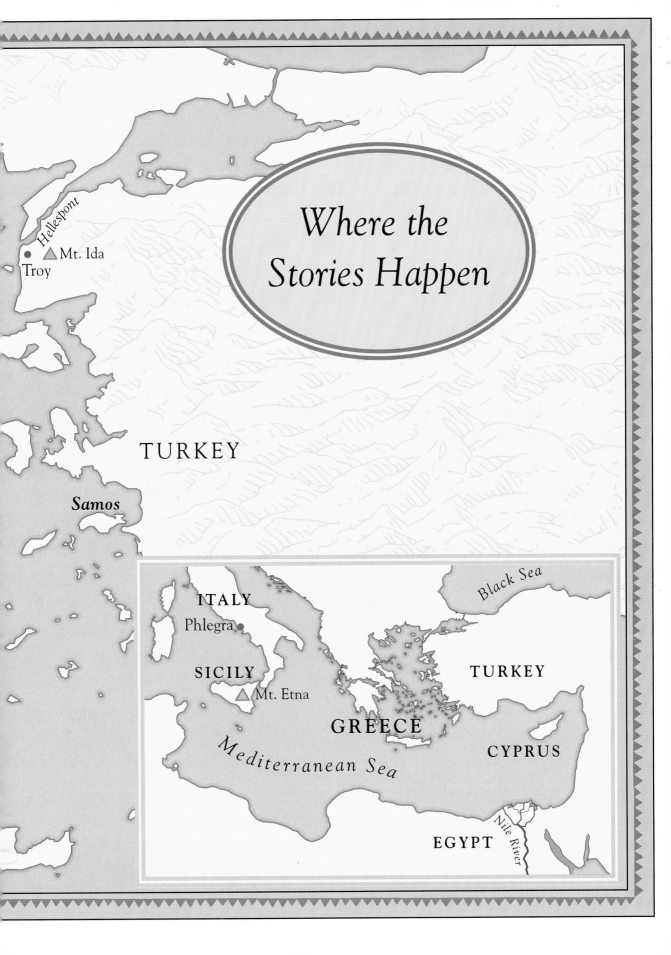

Hellespont

▲ Mt. Ida
● Troy

Where the Stories Happen

TURKEY

Samos

ITALY
Phlegra ●

SICILY
▲ Mt. Etna

Black Sea

TURKEY

GREECE

CYPRUS

Mediterranean Sea

EGYPT

Nile River

TO THE READER:

Just because the Introduction comes first doesn't mean you have to read it first. Start with any of the goddess stories. Read the Introduction anytime, starting with which- ever topic you prefer. But, please, save the Epilogue/Afterword for last.

INTRODUCTION

HOW GODDESSES AND GODS ARE DIFFERENT FROM HUMANS

They're immortal: They don't die. They don't grow old. Their faces are ideally beautiful and handsome. Their bodies are perfectly proportioned.

Most goddesses are taller and stronger than humans. How much taller, Hesiod and Homer (our best sources of information) don't disclose. We *do* know that Athena once snatched up Sicily—the whole island!—and hurled it at an enemy (see p. 89). So we can pretty well imagine how tall and strong she had to be when she accomplished such a feat.

At times the goddesses and gods dwindle to less imposing sizes. Some can shape-shift: Zeus famously appeared as bull, swan, quail, and golden shower. Athena liked to turn herself into a swallow, and she often took on human form.

They have a radiance around them, but can dim it anytime they please.

They can travel through the air—in chariots, on winged sandals, wind-propelled, or driven by sheer will.

Many of them live in palaces on the peaks of Mount Olympus and in the surrounding sky. Some also have homes down on earth. Hades lives in the Underworld; Poseidon, at the bottom of the sea.

They don't eat earthly food (although they sometimes make exceptions). They do enjoy the meat of animals roasting on their altars, but only after sacred fire turns it into fragrant plumes of smoke.

Their food is ambrosia, inestimably more delicious than anything we humans taste. It renews their immortality. Doves come flying daily, bringing fresh supplies to Mount Olympus.

On occasion, they drink water, also wine. But their celestial drink is nectar, which renews their youth.

Ichor (I-kor) flows through their veins; it is a liquid much like blood, save that it is eternal.

Their powers are great, but limited. No god or goddess can undo what another has brought about. If they defy the will of Zeus, he punishes them. And even Zeus is not all-powerful but is subject to Fate's decrees.

They can, and do, experience injuries and pain.

Because their time is endless they worry less about its passing than we humans do. Whether immortality heightens or lessens the meaningfulness of their lives, we may speculate about, but can never know.

WHO'S OLYMPIAN, WHO'S NOT?

The ancient Greeks believed that Gaia (GAH-yah, Earth) was the first, the oldest goddess. She created Uranus (you-

RAY-nus, Sky) to be her mate. They had many offspring, including the next generation of gods and goddesses, called Titans and Titanesses.

Titans		*Titanesses*	
Oceanus	(o-shee-AH-nus)	Tethys	(TETH-iss)
Hyperion	(hy-PEER-ee-on)	Theia	(THAY-ah)
Iapetus	(yah-PEET-us)	Themis	(THEM-iss)
Crius	(KRY-us)	Mnemosyne	(mee-MO-sin-ee)
Coeus	(KO-ee-us)	Phoebe	(FEE-bee)
Cronos	(KRO-nos)	Rhea	(RAY-ah)

They mated (not "married," because, as Hera will later explain, there was no such thing as marriage yet). They had many children. For instance: Hyperion and Theia had Helios, Selene, and Eos (sun, moon, and dawn). Tethys and Oceanus had all the river gods, and Metis (you'll meet her in Athena's story). Cronos and Rhea had six children: Hestia, Demeter, Hades, Poseidon, Hera, and Zeus.

Cronos was the youngest son of Gaia and Uranus. He overthrew his father, and made himself god-king of the world.

Zeus was the youngest son of Rhea and Cronos. He followed his father's example, and overthrew him. That ended the rule of Titan Cronos. Now Zeus was god-king of the world.

Zeus married Hera. (That's when marriage began.) He built palaces on Mount Olympus; called himself Olympian Zeus; and granted Olympian status to his sisters, to one brother, and to seven of the countless children he had fathered.

That made twelve Olympians, counting himself and Hera.

Olympian goddesses		*Olympian gods*	
Hera	(HEE-rah)	Zeus	(zooss)
Hestia	(HES-tee-ah)	Poseidon	(po-SY-don)
Demeter	(de-MEET-er)	Apollo	(a-POL-o)
Athena	(a-THEEN-ah)	Ares	(AH-rayz)
Aphrodite	(af-ro-DY-tee)	Hermes	(HER-meez)
Artemis	(AR-te-mis)	Dionysus	(dy-o-NY-sus)

You might wonder, Why did Zeus pick his one brother, Poseidon, but not his other brother, Hades? Because Hades lives down in the Underworld? And why, of Zeus's two sons by Hera, did he pick Ares, but not Hephaestus? Because Hephaestus limps, and isn't handsome? Or was Zeus just playing favorites? Well, no one ever said that Zeus is always just or fair.

However, he is generous, and hospitable. He welcomes gods and goddesses to visit Mount Olympus. He invites them, "Stay and feast with us." Then the immortals, all together, raise their cups, rejoice in being young forever, and it hardly matters who is an Olympian, who not.

WHAT WE OWE THE ANCIENT GREEKS

Theater and poetry; art and architecture; history; math; biology and other -ologies; philosophy; the idea of human freedom; democracy—if this list went on for twenty pages, it would barely scratch the surface of what began in ancient Greece and was passed along.

I hope you'll want to find out more about this astonishing, rich legacy. It inspired future cultures, including ours. But it had its underside, which also left its mark on future cultures, and which scholars didn't write about until quite recently: slavery, for instance; and how women were regarded.

WHAT LIFE WAS LIKE FOR GIRLS AND WOMEN

Let's start with Pandora. She's the first woman, and she started all the trouble in the world.

Here's how Hesiod told the myth, around 750 B.C.: Long ago "the race of men" lived happily on their own. Prometheus (pro-MEETH-ee-us), a lesser god, had formed the first man out of clay, and the race proliferated, more men appearing out of the ground as the old died off. Then, one day, Prometheus gave them fire, stolen from the sun. Zeus got angry with men for accepting this gift. He punished them by creating Pandora, lovely on the outside, but savage and wild inside. He sent her down to earth. Even more dangerous than the box of ills she came with, she herself was the source of woe to men.

Furthermore, she passed her vileness down to the entire female race. Men, beware, was Hesiod's warning; keep your wives and daughters in their places, under strict control.

That is what Greek men did.

They decided girls and women were incapable of reasoning (though Plato, for one, disagreed). Girls shouldn't go to school (except in Sparta). Female bodies were incurably weak (again, except in Sparta). Girls and women were excluded from the Olympics and from many other competitions—even the *Panathenaea,* held in Athena's honor, and no one saw the irony in that.

Women were not citizens (except in a myth about a bygone age, see pp. 23-26). They could not own property. Rather, they *were* property: fathers married off their daughters in exchange for cattle, sheep, or land. Women's functions were to oversee the household, make clothing, and raise children. And they were expected to behave demurely, not call attention to themselves.

Of course this is not the whole story. Certain women did have influence in important ways, as Sophocles' *Antigone,* or any play by any of the dramatists, makes eloquently clear. Still, it's fair to say that girls and women were treated unfairly, deprived of opportunities and rights we take for granted, and that they lived constricted lives.

RIGHT AND WRONG — MORAL VALUES, THEIRS AND OURS

Let's say you're a boy growing up in Athens around 450 B.C. You're with your *paedagogus* (py-dah-GO-gus). He's walking you to school. Let's see what customs and moral values this entails.

First, you're lucky, for two reasons:

1) You're lucky you're a boy. Girls didn't go to school, missed out on nearly everything, were considered inferior—and that wasn't considered unfair!

2) You're lucky to be growing up at all. Many babies,

sickly or unwanted, were "exposed"—left out in a field or on a mountain to starve and freeze. This was often done, and nobody deplored it.

Your *paedagogus* is a nanny-tutor. He shepherds you to school and to the *palaestra* (a pre-gym where you train for the real *gymnasium*). He is educated, helps you with your homework. Is he a servant? Yes, but not a paid one. He's a slave.

Slaves in Athens swept the streets, disposed of trash, did all the menial, necessary jobs. Thereby they freed the citizens to do the work of running the city-state.

In Athens, instead of electing representatives, as we do, all the citizens took turns making laws, enforcing them, and administering justice.

A democracy that values freedom, but has slaves? Isn't that incongruous? Yes, if you believe "that all men are created equal." But that idea only got started in the eighteenth century A.D.

The ancient Greeks believed in Fate. Fate earmarks certain people to be free and others to be slaves. This belief made slavery all right, and even fair. Here's how it works: You go to war, and if you win, you enslave your enemy. If you lose, well, then the shackle's on the other foot, and *you're* the one enslaved.

In your Athenian school, along with arithmetic, grammar, and music (considered very important in building character), these are some ideas you're learning about right and wrong, and how to live your life:

Youth is sweet, old age is bitter; life is short, and it's over when it's over. In the afterlife your shade wanders aimlessly through the Underworld, not remembering or feeling anything. Therefore, you had better make the most of your life while you're alive, and of inborn abilities—exert your body and your mind; become what you were meant to be; gain fulfillment while you can.

Be noble, brave, and daring like the heroes in Homer's *Iliad* and *Odyssey* (of which you'd be required to know great chunks by heart). Do great deeds in war. In peacetime, do your share of civic duties. Act justly, reasonably, wisely. Don't be arrogant.

Strive for honor and renown, so that people in the future will remember you and praise you. Therein lies your hope for immortality.

But your Athenian teachers aren't telling you, Be good; be kind; don't hurt other people's feelings. These were *not* among the virtues that Athenians cherished.

Also, their sense of wrong was different from ours. If a wrongful act was done—say, a murder—it caused *miasma* (my-AZ-mah), a pollution, and it had to be atoned in a public, formal way. They did not think in terms of sin. Their chief god had other matters on his mind than examining their consciences and souls.

ZEUS — GOOD GOD, BAD GOD, OR WHAT?

Picture a snow white bull, all sleek, down by the sea. It's Zeus. And a young princess, her name is Europa. She's playing in the sand. Bull-Zeus approaches. He nuzzles her. She strokes his cheek. He bends his forelegs, kneels.

His eyes say, Climb on me. She does. He gives a loud, triumphant bellow, leaps into the waves, and swims away with her.

That's the kind of god he is. Even as a bull, he's irresistible. In his own shape, he is vigorous, good-looking, sometimes rough and sometimes tender—the ultimate, the quintessential male.

Zeus is *not* a world creator. The world was already there. He merely took it over, by vanquishing its former ruler Cronos, his father.

And he didn't create humans—just Pandora, the first woman.

Zeus wields enormous power but is *not* almighty. Even he must bow to Fate, which is personified as three grim goddesses—Clotho (KLO-tho, "the spinner"), Lachesis (lah-KAY-sis, "the drawing of lots"), and Atropos (AH-trop-os, "inevitable").

As world ruler, Zeus must reckon with the chance that some new god—perhaps a son (he has many sons and daughters)—might try to overthrow him.

As weather god, he gathers clouds, commands the winds, and hurls thunderbolts. As sky god, he keeps order on Olympus: He presides at feasts and councils; settles deities' disputes. As faithless-husband god, he keeps an eye out for new lovers to pursue.

In his spare time, what does he do for humans?

A myth tells of two jars beside his door. One jar holds good things; the other, bad. And Zeus distributes these, but casually.

Humans aren't his prime concern. He insists that they

observe the basic rules: offer sacrifices; be hospitable; bury their dead; and avoid comparing themselves to gods. Beyond that, he doesn't care who does right or wrong.

He is a god who does whatever he pleases.

Some scholars put it this way: Zeus lives exactly how the humans who imagined him might have wished that *they* could live—eternally, and with impunity.

HOW AND WHY I WROTE THIS BOOK

First I met with three young girls I knew: Cara, Beth, and Rachel (not their real names), ages eleven, twelve, thirteen. I wanted to discover how they felt about mythology.

Cara started: "It bugs me when authors use old-fashioned language just to give you the idea that the myths are from ancient times."

Beth and Rachel agreed that the writing should sound natural, not stuffy, but not slangy, either.

I asked them why they thought Greek myths have been retold so often and still are popular.

Because they're exciting, with lots of action and few boring stretches when nothing's happening, my consultants said.

We talked about goddesses. They thought Athena was awesome; Aphrodite, amazing; and they did *not* like Hera.

"But it's unfair that *she* gets blamed for being the possessive, jealous wife, and Zeus gets away with being unfaithful, having lots of love affairs, and no one blames *him*," Rachel said.

This led to a lively discussion about attitudes toward women, then and now.

Toward the end of our meeting I asked, "What do you like *best* about myths?"

"That anything can happen," Cara answered. "Like, Zeus can be a cuckoo, and a horse can fly. It's cool. You never know what's coming next."

Next I asked, "What do you like *least?*"

"That anything can happen," Cara answered with equal conviction. "Because it can't, in real life. So you can't relate to the characters it happens to."

The others nodded.

Rachel said, "I mind that myths don't let you in on the characters' private thoughts. So you don't get to know them that well."

"And you can't get as emotionally involved with them as you do with characters in novels," Beth added.

"Yes, but still, I love goddess stories," Cara said. "They give me a special feeling, I mean, a kind of *glow.* . . ."

I'd taken notes, but hardly needed them. My consultants' comments stayed clearly in my mind, and helped me as I worked.

In my reading—Homer, Hesiod, Virgil, Ovid, and later myth retellings—I'd come across more incidents about Athena, Aphrodite, and Hera than I could ever possibly retell. Besides, the ancient sources often disagree. (For instance, Hesiod's Aphrodite was born of sea foam, but in Homer she's the daughter of Zeus and the little-known goddess Dione!) Which ones should I choose?

I mulled them over, gave them room in my imagination.

Eventually certain incidents *felt* right. Then my task was to combine the incidents sequentially into *story* order (which required groping my way through the blurry timelessness of myth to try and sort out what happened when); and to build three separate, but connected narratives.

My hope was that, if I worked well, each goddess would reveal herself in undiminished splendor, with her personality as fascinating now as it was in classic times.

Working well meant keeping faith with my sources: staying true to Hesiod and Homer (who "wrote the book" on ancient Greek beliefs), even while I made the leaps required to stir the emotions and imaginations of present-day young readers.

All along, I listened for Athena's voice, and Aphrodite's, Hera's, in the way that writers listen, as I'd always listened before when trying to get inside fictional characters' heads. It had worked with *human* characters. But these were goddesses. . . . That gave me pause. It seemed a nervy undertaking. And was it even nervier to write their stories in *their* voices?

Every generation can only tell the ancient myths anew out of its own needs and concerns, and in its own writing styles. Hesiod and Homer (whom nobody called nervy!) claimed to be writing down *verbatim* what the Muses (goddesses!) personally sang into their human ears. And Virgil claimed it too, eight hundred years later, when hardly anyone believed in the Muses anymore, at least not literally. I thought about all that, and gave myself permission to go ahead and give my goddesses their say.

When I was eleven or twelve I fell in love with every-body up on Mount Olympus, especially the goddesses. Athena lent me courage to be brainy, although I was a girl. Aphrodite, queen of love, romance, and everything I lay awake nights trying to imagine, thrilled me to the core. Hera I disliked, of course. The myths I read all said she was a shrew. And no girl back then (it was long ago) would have thought to argue, Yes, but Zeus was bad to her. . . .

Anyway, I wanted, needed, *craved* more goddess stories. I hung around the library, hoping every day some myth book I hadn't read yet would turn up. And I wished its title would be *Goddesses of Ancient Greece*.

That never happened. All the goddess stories—too few! too short!—were tucked away in books with male *Gods-and-Heroes* kinds of titles. We girls got the message: Females, even goddesses, don't rate titles of their own.

That's how it was. That's how it stayed. To the best of my knowledge, this is the only book exclusively about the goddesses of ancient Greece.

I wrote my book to fill this need, and because, in Cara's words, "I still love goddess stories. They give me a special feeling, I mean, a kind of *glow*."

ATHENA, APHRODITE, HERA —
WHY THESE THREE?

Each goddess is unique in her appeal.

Athena's brilliance gives the lie to the idea that *female*

means *unreasonable*. She can reason rings around every god on Mount Olympus! As for her choice of virginity, it's not that she dislikes male company. She's fond of many gods and of heroic men. It's just that rather than devote herself to lovers, she invests her energies in her inventions; in her heroes, helping them win battles; and in championing her city, Athens.

Aphrodite—perfect beauty, sexy love, enchantment. Who wouldn't thrill to enter her domain?

Hera—well, Zeus plays around, and *she* gets blamed for being jealous! It's time to give this goddess credit. She knows something about love that Aphrodite doesn't know: Marriage can make love stronger. Hera's love withstands betrayals. She holds her marriage sacred, thereby suggesting an ideal to which all spouses can aspire.

These goddesses, each so sharply different from the other two, are linked together by intense emotions they feel for one another.

In one story sequence, all three goddesses are rivals, fiercely competing for the golden apple (see pp. 41 and 51-54). In all the rest, Athena and Hera get along, are devoted to each other. And they both don't like Aphrodite, who, in turn, dislikes them both. That makes Athena and Hera even better friends.

Their situation struck me as the goddess version of what often happens among girls: Three live in proximity. Two are close. The one who's left out pretends not to mind, but she finds ways to spite the other two. This intrigued me, and I wanted to explore it.

Finally, Athena, Aphrodite, and Hera represent such

contrasting styles of being female, I felt that each could be imagined fullest in conjunction and comparison with the other two.

THE PARADOX: EXALTED GODDESSES, DEBASED WOMEN

Paradox—I looked it up. "From Greek, *paradoxos*, conflicting with expectation," my dictionary says.

Ancient Greece honored its goddesses and treated women not much better than slaves—yes, that *does* conflict with expectation.

It is a glaring contradiction.

Yet, classics scholars writing earlier than 1980 didn't even mention, much less question, it.

Scholars writing since the eighties give two explanations. First, the ancient Greeks made a categorical distinction between goddesses and mortal females, considering them as unrelated species. You may not find this too convincing, especially when you look at any classical goddess statue and note how very woman-like or young-girl-like, only still more beautiful, it is.

Second, some anthropologists and mythologists believe that powerful goddesses are remnants of a much more ancient culture that was ruled by *women* and in which *men* were oppressed. Later men rebelled and took over. According to this theory, misogyny (mis-AH-jin-ee—hating and debasing women) conceals men's deep-rooted fear that women might rise up and take men's power away.

This theory has never been proved.

Someday someone—maybe you—will resolve the paradox. In the meantime, here is what it says to me:

How women were treated in ancient Greece tells only half, the bad half, of the story. The other half, the shining half about the goddesses, holds out this vision: Women—the mortal counterparts of goddesses—and men embracing as equals; misogyny fading into the dim past.

WE GODDESSES

ATHENA

You say I'm Zeus's brainchild? You think that he alone gave me my birth, and made me wise?

✤ Listen. I will tell you how it was:

A dark space enclosed me. The bigger I grew, the more its circular wall confined me.

Then came groans, and cries of pain, then thunderous blows crashed down.

Suddenly brightness flashed before my eyes.

Metis (MAY-tiss, "thought").

"It's the light of day, my darling!" Metis spoke these words to me. Her name means "thought." She was, she is the wisest goddess. With her begins my story.

Hera (HEE-rah) is queen of the gods.

My father loved her long before he married Hera—and long after, too.

It was after Zeus had married that he got Metis with child.

"This child will be a daughter," the earth's most sacred oracle promised. "But, Zeus, be warned: If Metis bears you another child, that one will be a son. And that son will overthrow you, as you did *your* father."

Titans (TY-tonz) sprang from Gaia (GAH-yah, Earth) and Uranus (yoo-RAY-nus, Sky). They are ancestors of the Olympian gods and goddesses (Zeus, Hera, etc.).

True, Zeus had overthrown *his* father, Cronos, the Titan god-king who had ruled the world before.

Zeus wondered, What should I do? He found Metis so alluring that he could not trust himself to keep from fathering another child on her. Shall I banish her to some place far? . . . I mustn't let her stay, yet I don't want to lose her. . . .

There's only one way out . . . or rather, *in*. . . . He took a deep, long breath. Then, with one tremendous gust, he blew out all the air from inside his chest and belly. Good, now there was room.

He dropped his jaw to his chin, opened his mouth wide, wide, grabbed hold of Metis—and swallowed her down into himself.

This is the secret that tellers of my story hide:

Metis was, and is, my mother. I, Athena, am the daughter she carried in her womb. They lie who say I sprang from Zeus alone.

Inside Zeus's belly, Metis gave me birth.

She touched her lips to my eyelids. "May vision fill your eyes." She touched her fingers to the sides of my head. "May thought bring understanding to your mind." She touched the tips of her fingers to mine. "May *techne* flow into your hands."

Thus she gave me vision, understanding, skill.

My mother's threefold gift grants me the power to envision new, astonishing devices; to understand how they must work; and to bring them into being.

As surely as Atlas holds up the sky, and Eos brings each day its dawn, I, Athena—thanks to *techne*—invented all of these:

The trumpet, to blare forth triumphant deeds. The plow, to dig furrows in fields. The yoke, to harness oxen. The

Techne (TEK-nay) in Greek means "skill" or "craft." We get such words as technical and technique from it.

Atlas (AT-las, "he who carries"), a Titan, carries the sky, holding it up on his shoulders.

Eos (EE-os), goddess of dawn, is the sister of Helios (HEE-lee-os), the sun god, and of Selene (se-LEE-nee), moon goddess.

chariot, for driving into battle. The ship, to carry voyagers over the sea's stormy back.

The loom, and how to weave on it—or else we'd still be wearing the scratchy hides of animals for clothing.

Yes, and the bridle, for taming horses. And the chisel, with which I sculpted the first statue in the world . . .

✦ My mother Metis suckled me till I was strong, then helped me struggle upward, into Zeus's head.

There I grew, till Zeus came down to earth one day, to stroll along the pleasant bank of the river Triton. It was then his head began to throb. And he cried out for help.

Gods and goddesses rushed down from Mount Olympus. The smith god Hephaestus brought his hammer and beat on Zeus's head, blow upon blow.

The wall around me quaked and shook.

"Be calm," said my mother, reaching up from deep in Zeus's belly. "Fear nothing."

One last, loudest blow crashed down. A rift sprang open, letting daylight in.

My mother pushed hard on the soles of my feet, helping me to climb out, and said, "Go now. Live in the light forever."

"Mother, come with me!"

"I cannot. Zeus needs my presence inside him, to put wisdom in his mind."

She lifted me up. I squeezed myself through. At once, the rift closed over, and Zeus felt no more pain.

❖

Zeus (zooss) needs no wings or chariot, but strides through the sky to get where he wants to go.

Triton (TRY-ton) is a mythical river, as well as the name of its god.

Hephaestus (he-FES-tus), son of Zeus and Hera, crafts the Olympians' weapons, armor, and jewelry and makes their chariots, too.

✦ The story has it that I wore armor, brandished a spear—true. But some say I emerged full-grown—not so. I was a child.

I shouted with glee at the spaciousness and brightness all around.

"This is my newest daughter, sprung from my head," Zeus proclaimed.

The gods cheered loudly and congratulated him.

The goddesses cheered too, but not as loudly. And Hera, Zeus's wife, cheered not at all.

Zeus stood me on his shoulders. "See how her golden armor shines! Is my daughter not wonderful?"

"Yes, wonderful," they all exclaimed.

Hephaestus pointed a sooty finger at me. "*I* delivered her. Now, Zeus, pay me my midwife fee: Say you'll let me marry her as soon as she grows up."

I knew nothing of the world yet, only that I'd never want to marry. "No!" I cried out, very loud.

Zeus laughed. "Stand back, Hephaestus. You have my thanks; that's pay enough." Then he proclaimed his hopes and plans for me:

"Athena will be wise and strong. She'll fight beside many great heroes. She will lend them strength and cunning, help them slay voracious monsters.

"Athena will thrill to the clash and clangor of arms." He grasped my wrist in his huge hand, and guiding my spear, he jabbed and stabbed the air. "She will prevail in many a bloody campaign. Poets will sing of her victories for as long as time endures—"

"What shall I do in peacetime, Father?"

He wrinkled his brows as though angry that I'd interrupted, but then he grinned and said proudly, "You are bold, my Athena, you'll do noble deeds that will make the whole world glad. . . ." He paused, perhaps to listen to ideas my mother, Metis, sent into his mind.

"I know a city," he continued. "It's in the heart of Attica, which is in the heart of sacred Greece—"

Athens. You'll hear more about it later.

"You promised that city to *me*!" exclaimed a god with a dark blue, wavy beard, and seaweed in his hair. This was Poseidon. He brandished his three-pronged spear. "Zeus, don't you remember? You apportioned *me* that city in the heart of Greece, when you divided up the lands and places of the earth."

Poseidon (po-sy-don), Zeus's brother, is the ruler of the sea.

Zeus answered, "Yes, but that was before Athena was born."

"Just the same, is not your word law? And you *said*—"

"Well, *now* I say, you have a rival: Athena, my new daughter. Hear my will, Poseidon: You each shall do the city a service. Whoever does the greater service will be the city's champion." Zeus gave my hand a little squeeze to let me know he hoped it would be me. "Either way, the city will be famous, the foremost city of men."

This perplexed me, and I asked, "Won't women live there too, and children?"

"Yes, of course." Now Zeus grew impatient, swung me down, and spoke grandly on, not *to*, but *about* me, as though I were not there: "My new and glorious daughter will counsel me in all great matters. I'll share the power of my *aegis* with her. She will be second only to me. All you gods will hold her in highest esteem."

The aegis (EE-jiss) is a shield, covered with goatskin. It has a fringe of snakes, and Medusa's (me-DOO-sah) head is in the middle.

Themis (THEM-iss).

Feeling even more perplexed, I asked the goddesses, "Why just the gods? Won't *you* esteem me, too?"

They laughed at my questions. "How little she knows," said one.

"She has a lot to learn," another said.

"What do you mean?" A new emotion—anger—made my cheeks grow hot. "What have I said to make you laugh?"

They wouldn't answer.

Finally Themis—she's the goddess of politeness!—said rudely, "You're so ignorant! When Zeus says *gods*, it's just a way of speaking. He means us, too, that's understood."

"Well, *I* don't understand it. Isn't it discourteous to leave out mentioning us?"

"That's the way it is," Themis said, and shrugged.

I didn't like it. I went down to the riverbank and threw pebbles in the water.

Hera came and sat near me. I thought, since she was Zeus's wife, perhaps she wished *she* could have been my mother. In any case, she looked unhappy. Or maybe she was thirsty.

I scooped up sparkling river water. She drank it from my hands and took me on her lap.

We sat together, chatting. Then Zeus approached. He pulled me to my feet and said, "Athena, dear, of all my children, even those not born as yet, you will always be my favorite. I will always keep you by my side."

✦ Yes, but by "always" he meant later, when I would be grown.

As sky king, with the whole world to rule, Zeus had no

time to care for a small child. I thought perhaps he would ask Hera to care for me and be my foster mother. But she flashed him an angry look and stalked away.

"Is there a shepherd hereabouts?" he shouted, making himself heard far and wide. "Or a kindly goatherd or good farmwife who'll raise this child for me?"

No such person came.

But the river waters parted, revealing a brawny figure shaped like a man, with a fish's tail below. Beads of water sparkled in his green hair and wavy beard. He was Triton, the river's god.

Mythic river gods went by the same names as their rivers.

He balanced himself on a rock, and the waters joined back together.

Then pearl-like bubbles as though of someone's breath appeared, and a pair of shining eyes, round and wide apart, looked up at me. . . . Or were those my own eyes, that the river and the light reflected back?

I looked down at the water again and saw only grasses drifting by.

"With just this one pleasant river to rule, I have not much to do," Triton said. "Great Zeus, I'll gladly raise your child for you."

"Thank you, gracious river god," my father answered.

I kept gazing at the water, wishing that the face would reappear.

When I looked up, I saw the air aglow with radiance as the gods and goddesses soared away, my father leading them back to their dwellings on high.

Triton unfastened the golden shin guards I had on. "Little Athena, be happy here with us," he said.

Shin guards, also called greaves, are part of the armor that warriors wear.

He took me into the water. He clapped his hands. At

once the river girl whose eyes I'd seen rose up and stood before me.

"This is my daughter, Pallas. You'll be playfellows. Come." Triton led the way down to their home, built of spacious caverns deep in the riverbed.

He was the kindest foster father, as loving to me as to his own child. He taught us all the fishes' names; took us to visit wood nymphs in their tree homes on the banks; showed us how to blow on conch shells (which Pallas learned better than I). He warned us against riding the wild river horses, but did not scold us harshly when we rode them all the same.

As for Pallas, no one ever had a livelier, more congenial friend. Slender but sturdy, not with a fish tail but with legs like mine, she was curious, high-spirited, as brave as I, and brimming with ideas for bold adventures.

We raced on foot, on land, and on our backs or bellies in the river. We held underwater contests. I'd stay submerged until I sputtered and had to gasp for air. But Pallas could breathe in the water, so she always won.

We followed the river to the mountain where it was born as a silver waterfall. We scrambled to the top and came sliding, bouncing, somersaulting down.

One day we played that we were warrior chiefs. Our opposing armies had fought too long, at too great cost. It was time we ended the conflict ourselves by fighting hand to hand.

We made ferocious faces, shouted strident battle cries. Our fists shot out, hers first, about to strike.

Just then Zeus looked down. (He often did, he later told me, to see that all was well with me.) He thought

Nymphs are lesser goddesses. Some are immortal. Others can live for centuries, but then they die.

we were in earnest. He feared that I'd be harmed and threw down his *aegis* to protect me.

It landed between us with a heavy thud. Pallas stumbled and failed to deliver her blow. But I delivered mine. I hit her square in the chest, so hard I felt her flesh tear, heard her bones break. In my zeal to win our battle, I forgot the one way we were not alike:

Pallas had a human mother, therefore was mortal and could die.

She lay crumpled at my feet.

I threw myself down beside her. I blew my breath into her mouth, in vain.

We goddesses don't, cannot, weep. Our sorrows, it is said, are quickly over. But mine remained. My whole being thirsted, so parched were my eyes for sorrow-easing tears. I wished for what could never be: to die, in order that my shade could join the shade of Pallas. I called on Hermes. He is the god who leads the dead down to the Underworld. I begged him, "Lead me there."

"It is forbidden. Be glad that you're immortal. Zeus awaits you on Olympus." Hermes held out his hand to me. "Come."

No, I was not ready.

I walked up and down in the shallows of the river, aimless, waiting for my grief to lift. A chunk of wood drifted toward me. I picked it up. I rubbed it smooth, polished it with soft leaves till the lines and tracings in it shone. The way they caught the light reminded me of sunshine glinting on tendrils of Pallas's hair. And this notion came to me: Can I turn the wood into her likeness?

So then I made the implement that I would need for

The ancient Greeks believed that the dead, once buried, become shades or shadows of their former selves.

Hermes (HER-meez), a son of Zeus, is a messenger god and patron of travelers and thieves.

The Underworld is the realm of the dead, ruled by Hades.

carving: wooden handle, metal edge—a chisel, my first invention. I took a stone, used it as a cudgel to drive the chisel into the wood. And I carved and carved until I had the likeness of Pallas, limb for limb.

I hugged it to me, kissed it on the mouth, and swore, "Beloved friend, your name shall live forever."

And so it lives, for on that day I joined her name to mine: I am often called Pallas Athena.

I'd made the statue look as much like Pallas as I could. But in the act of sculpting, unknowingly I'd blended my own features in with hers. When I looked again, I saw a reminder of our friendship, of how close, how nearly one, we two had been.

I wanted Triton to have it.

But Triton said, "No statue can replace my child. You didn't mean to kill her. But leave me now. Farewell." And he wept so hard, his river overflowed.

Zeus sent his eagle for the statue. The great bird clutched it in his talons and with mighty wingbeats rose into the blue. For years and years I could not learn its whereabouts. My father would not speak of it.

He sent Hermes to the flooded riverbank for me.

Some sources say Zeus kept one huge eagle; others say, several; still others say that he himself became an eagle when he wanted somebody or something quickly snatched up from the earth.

✦ Hermes led me up into the sky. This was my first experience of gliding over clouds, rising effortlessly higher—oh, the wondrousness of it!

Soon we reached the gods' and goddesses' bright realm atop the sunlit peaks of Mount Olympus. Zeus himself flung wide the gates. "Athena, welcome."

He led me in. I assumed my rightful place as prized and

trusted daughter at his side. In time his hopes and plans for me came true:

I took part in his deliberations and I gave him counsel.

I thrilled to the clangor of weapons in wars. I fought alongside countless heroes. I'll tell you about three:

One was Cadmus. He set out to found the city of Thebes. When he got there, a dragon devoured his soldiers. Cadmus slew the dragon. But how was he to found a city all alone? "Pull out the dragon's teeth, and plant them," I advised. He looked puzzled, but obeyed. To his surprise, the teeth, turned into soldiers, leaped forth from the ground, and with their help he founded Thebes. Something else that Cadmus did was invent the alphabet. That, too, was my idea. I'm glad and proud I thought of it. For wouldn't it be tiresome if there were still no writing, and no reading?

Thebes (theebz), in Boeotia (bo-EE-shah), central Greece, was a leading city in antiquity.

Another of my heroes was Odysseus, king of Ithaca. I loved him best, because he had a supple mind and nimble wit. I inspired him to think up clever strategies. I shielded him from harm throughout the Trojan War and from many dangers on his long, hard voyage home.

Odysseus (o-DISS-ee-us) is the hero of Homer's Odyssey.

Ithaca (ITH-ah-kah) is an island off the northwest coast of Greece.

A third was Perseus, who battled Medusa, as you soon shall hear. . . .

First, though, what's heroic?

Being brave, you say?

Yes, but what is bravery?

Taking risks? Yes, I agree.

But what is bravest?

Risking your life. For that, you must be mortal. And heroes are.

Perseus (PER-see-us) is a son of Zeus and of Danae (DAH-nah-ee), the woman Zeus made love to disguised as a shower of gold.

That's why I love them. But not in Aphrodite's way, which ignites the senses and arouses craving. I'd never crave heroes for lovers, or indeed crave any lovers at all.

I guard against the lust the love goddess inspires. It was lust that made Hephaestus throw himself across my path as I headed for Zeus's council hall one morning. He clutched, he pinched and squeezed. I gave him one good push. He fell, crashed his head against a wall, and I was rid of him. But my body still remembers his hulking shape, his hungry groping hands. And I have no appetite for being grasped and mauled.

I want to stay a virgin and be like the city I champion: unassailable. When would-be invaders threaten, I defend it. The city's intactness and my own are one. And always I renew my pledge: No god or mortal man shall ever conquer me.

❧ Of the monsters my heroes defeated, there was one whom I myself made monstrous: Medusa. She was a Gorgon, but unlike her repulsive sisters, she was very pretty and seductive, with long, luxuriant hair.

Two Gorgon sisters, Stheno (STHEN-o) and Euryale (yu-RYE-ah-lee) are scary-looking sea creatures.

One day I visited a favorite temple of mine. The offerings of barley cakes and first fruits of the season had been pushed aside. Instead there lay Medusa consorting with her sea-god lover, none other than Poseidon, on *my* altar!

This outraged me so, I punished her at once: caused her tongue to swell into a bulbous lump; her teeth to grow jagged and crooked; her hair to turn into a mass of writhing serpents. I made her so chillingly hideous that whoever looked her in the face would turn to stone— but, in my haste, I failed to envision the consequence: I had made her invulnerable. She traveled the countryside wreaking destruction, rendering inanimate anyone who tried to stop her.

Finally along came Perseus, as fearless a hero as ever there was. *"I'll* stop Medusa," he vowed.

Hermes lent him winged sandals. The three Graiae, ancient, grizzled goddesses, lent him a cap that made him invisible.

The Graiae (GRY-eye) are three goddess sisters, born wrinkled, old, almost blind, with just one eye and just one tooth among them.

But neither cap nor sandals would prevent his turning to stone when he looked at Medusa, as he would have to do in order to strike at her. How to get around this?

Perseus had no idea. (Fearless heroes aren't all brilliant.)

But *I* knew a way.

Hephaestus, sorry for his rude behavior, had forged me a strong, smooth shield, and had made it mirror-bright, as I had asked him to.

I came to Perseus in a dream. (When goddesses or gods appear undisguised to mortals in their waking life, it can happen that our splendor overwhelms their eyes, and they go blind, or else they die.) In the dream I told him, "When you do battle with Medusa, look only at her mirror image, reflected in this shield."

When he awoke, the shield lay beside him.

Then we flew—he, on Hermes' sandals; I, as a swallow—to the land of the Gorgons, at the northernmost end of the earth. We found Medusa in a forest, sleeping.

She lay with her back to us. The serpents sprouting from her head slept also. And stones stood everywhere about. Some were in the shapes of beasts, but most were human.

Perseus hovered close above her.

"Now!" I urged.

He drew his sickle.

Medusa woke to its curved blade a hair's breadth away from her throat. The serpents woke with her. They darted their wedge-shaped heads at Perseus's heels. But he winged his way up beyond reach.

Medusa stretched forward, hands around her throat to protect it from the sickle, and chanted in a voice like ice and iron, "Invisible one, look at me!"

Perseus remembered to look only at the shield, and wielding the sickle with lightning speed, slashed her in the foot, the thigh, the small of the back, ever higher.

"Now in the heart!" I cried in my own voice.

Medusa's hands flew to her breast. But I had instructed Perseus that "in the heart" would mean "Cut her head off!"

Her throat now bare, Perseus's sickle sliced it through. Serpents lashed forward, breathing their last, as Medusa's head dropped to the ground.

Blood gushed upward from her neck.

From this crimson fountain a marvelous creature took form: pure white, with gleaming mane and silver moon-shaped hooves—Pegasus, the winged horse, fathered by Poseidon on Medusa in my temple. His nostrils quivered. He breathed his first breath. His hooves pawed the air, then he spurted off into the clouds.

✤ I willed myself after him and watched him gambol: He fluttered and bounced on air, then, with mighty wing beats, went spiraling up, swooped lower, and galloped from billow to billow.

Apollo, son of Zeus and Leto (LEE-toh), twin brother of Artemis, is an archer, dragon slayer, and god of the arts and medicine.

The nine Muses are the daughters of Zeus and Mnemosyne (nee-MO-sin-ee, goddess of memory) and are goddesses of the arts.

I held out my arms, "Come, little foal!"

He looked at me with lustrous eyes the color of the sea. "I'm wild as the winds, and I want to go where I wish," his high, clear whinny said.

I coaxed him with soft, clucking sounds. He approached. Cautiously I reached out my hand. He did not draw back but let me stroke his cheek and smooth his mane. I felt a sweet contentment, as though Pallas were beside me, as though we two together delighted in his company.

A shout cut short my reverie. "Welcome, Pegasus, at last!" Apollo came striding through a cloud. He is the god of prophecy. He had long known that such a horse would be born. And he knew where Pegasus was needed.

"You must take him to Mount Helicon," Apollo said to me. Mount Helicon is home to the Muses, and Apollo is their leader.

"Why? Haven't I a right to keep the horse? After all, he was begotten on *my* altar when Poseidon and Medusa defiled *my* temple with their lewd embraces."

"Yes. But if you bring him to Mount Helicon before the sun goes down, he will do a wonder there. Athena, please." Apollo's golden eyes beseeched me. I could not refuse.

The sun already stood low. Helicon was far, and Pegasus not tamed.

We were near Olympus. I went and fetched the bridle I'd invented. I'd braided it together of three pliant, gold-embroidered strips of leather, not knowing then what horse would wear it.

Pegasus flung his head from side to side and snorted. But seeing that I was determined, he took the bit into his mouth and let me fit the leather parts around his head.

I mounted and rode, firmly holding the reins. Alpine peaks glowed rosy in the late light; the sun was beginning to sink below the edge of the sky when Helicon came into view.

"Quick, Pegasus, fly down!" I pressed my knees against his sides. I pulled on the left rein, hard, to steer him to a landing spot. He faltered.

I slid forward, clung tight to his neck. Then—clash!— his metal hoof struck stone.

Pegasus found his footing. I dismounted.

The nine Muses came running and greeted us. Urania hung a garland of fresh-picked flowers around the horse's neck.

"Look!" cried Calliope, pointing to the ground.

At my feet lay two round segments of the rock that Pegasus's silver hoof had broken. Water seeped up, slowly at first, then flowed freely from a spring as clear as dew.

Clio dipped her finger in, and spoke to it: "Be known as Hippocrene, the horse's spring, for Pegasus created you when his hoof struck the rock."

"Well named," Apollo said, appearing in the Muses' midst. "Let us taste how fresh the water is."

The Muses drank from it.

"Athena, you, too." Apollo bent down, filled his hand with water, and put it to my lips.

It tasted almost like the nectar, indescribably delicious, that we immortals drink.

Urania (yoo-RAY-nee-ah, "heavenly") is the Muse of astronomy.

Calliope (kah-LY-o-pee, "fair voice") is the Muse of epic poetry.

Clio (KLEE-oh, "renown"), is the Muse of history.

Euterpe (yoo-TER-pee, "glad-ness") is the Muse of flute playing.

Thalia (thah-LEE-ah, "good cheer") is the Muse of comedy.

Melpomene (mel-POM-e-nee, "singing") is the Muse of tragedy.

Erato (e-RAH-to, "lovely") is the Muse of lyric poetry.

Polymnia (Po-LIM-nee-ah, "many songs") is the Muse of singing.

Terpsichore (terp-SIK-o-ree, "joy in the dance") is the Muse of dancing.

Demeter (de-MEET-er, "bar-ley mother") is the goddess who makes fields be fertile and yield crops.

Euterpe played her double flute. Thalia put on her comic mask. Melpomene, Erato, and Polymnia sang. Terpsichore led them all in a new dance.

I was never known for nimble feet or tuneful voice, but I joined in. Having sipped the water from the spring, I found that I could dance quite prettily, and sing on key, for once.

"Well done," Apollo said. "We thank you, Pegasus."

We thank him still, and always shall. For the water from the spring that Pegasus let flow inspires the Muses. And they in turn inspire poets, dance and music makers, all who add to beauty and enjoyment in the world.

❖ Poseidon, just as Zeus had willed, became my rival over the Attic city in the heart of Greece. He hated me from far, far back.

And just like Pegasus, Poseidon, too, caused a spring to flow, though of a different sort. . . .

Zeus had given Hades the Underworld, and Poseidon the sea to rule. But Poseidon was restless, not content to stay in his watery domain. He liked to roam about on land and wished the bottom of the sea were tillable, could yield good crops of grain.

One day he wandered through a rocky meadow where Demeter and I were playing. This was soon after I'd left Triton's river. I had not forgotten Pallas, and I never will. But Demeter's companionship—she was a girlish goddess then—gave me some ease from grieving.

Demeter leaned her face against a tree to give me time to hide. I ran and crouched behind a boulder.

"Here I come," she called, and started seeking.

It was then Poseidon saw her. He was struck with wanting to possess her and begged, "Lovely goddess, marry me!"

Demeter taunted him. "Oh, I couldn't. I'm too young. Besides, think of your wife, Amphitrite. Yet tell me, I'd just like to know, what would you give me?"

Amphitrite (am-fi-TRY-tee) is the goddess of the sea.

"What *wouldn't* I?" Poseidon took her question for encouragement. He sat himself down and patted his knee, wanting her to sit there.

She wouldn't, but sat next to him.

"You've heard of the devilfish? It's an evil, bloblike beast with a sac for a body and eight tentacles that suck the life out of its victims. And you've heard of the squid, all mouth and *ten* such tentacles? *I* created those, and other such, out of my teeming imagination," Poseidon boasted, leaving out that he'd done so for Amphitrite's entertainment.

Demeter shuddered.

"I'll tell you what: I'll make an animal, just for you, right now. It will be as pleasing as my sea creatures are ugly—perfectly proportioned and patient, willing to be ridden. You will love it, I assure you—" Poseidon looked dreamy, imagining the new creature's flawlessness.

He set to work: dug up great chunks and clumps of earth, stomped on them, molded them between his hands, murmuring rhymes all the while, but also stealing glances at Demeter—her face, her hair, her long legs stretched out before him.

"It's starting to move. My creature is coming alive," he cried, excited. "Demeter, look!"

I looked, too, peeking out from behind my boulder,

at an astonishing creature struggling to its feet. It was mottled, brown with irregular spots, had a quite long neck, a dainty face, and two little horns on top of its head.

Its spindly legs kept growing, even as we watched. Soon its knobby knees were level with the top of my boulder. And still its legs grew and grew—but not as long as its neck, at the end of which its face looked comically small.

Its tongue was very long, too; pink on top, black on the underside. The creature stuck it out and used it to pluck a leaf from the top of a very tall tree.

"It's wonderfully different," Demeter granted, "but 'perfectly proportioned,' did you say?"

The giraffe—for that's what it was—heard Demeter laugh. Perhaps that hurt its feelings, or else it was shy. In any case, it bolted away.

Poseidon was mortified. "That's not what I meant at all! Your loveliness distracted me. Sweet Demeter, I beg you, let me try again! I'll tell you what: To honor and to please you, I'll make the creature's pelt as milk white as your tunic. Or shall I make it raven black, the color of your hair?"

Demeter said, "As you wish."

Poseidon set to work, touching her hair, toying with the hem of her tunic while he molded, rhyming, humming to himself. This time he came closer to his goal: created an animal quite well proportioned, though rather stout, with a broad back and bristly mane, and a pelt that was neither black nor white but dizzyingly striped in both.

"I like it," said Demeter, to be polite, and held out her hand to touch it.

But the zebra, as the creature came to be called, bared its big teeth, made a neighing noise that meant, You'd better not ride on *me*, and went galloping away.

"One more try! Please, just one more try!" Poseidon begged.

And she said, "All right."

But he was so ashamed, and so distracted, that this time he came up with a shaggy beast that looked demure but spat great gobs of spittle, had an unshapely hump on its back, and swayed like a ship in the wind when it walked.

Demeter laughed aloud. So did I. Poseidon heard me, dragged me out from behind my boulder, and was furious with me.

He finally succeeded: created the horse, as he'd intended. But he never forgave me for watching him try three times and fail.

✤ About the spring Poseidon caused to flow:

The time came for that Attic city Zeus had spoken of to choose which of us two should be its champion.

Poseidon took the first turn rendering a service to the city.

He climbed its highest hill, called the Acropolis. When he reached the pinnacle, he thrust his trident hard into the rock.

Water spewed out.

"There. I've given you a spring!" Poseidon shouted proudly. "Now, citizens, make me your champion god."

The city's men, and women, too—yes, women were citizens in that time!—climbed up to see the spring.

It was murky, brackish, and had a briny smell. "What good is such water?" the men and women grumbled.

Acropolis (ah-KROP-o-lis) means "top of the city." The marks Poseidon's three-pronged trident left in the rock could still be seen some thousand years later, in Roman times.

Next it was my turn. And I planted a tree. Its branches grew in graceful curves, its leaves flashed silver in the sun, and it covered itself with countless small, oval-shaped fruits. It was the world's first olive tree.

Even before the olives ripened and yielded their rich, golden oil, the citizens agreed that they preferred my olive tree to Poseidon's spring.

But they had learned, from earthquakes and sea storms Poseidon had sent them in the past, that it was dangerous to offend him.

They assembled in their meeting hall. They debated what to do. Finally, they put the question to a vote.

All the men, it so happened, voted that Poseidon be their champion. The women all voted for me.

There was one more woman present than there were men. I was voted champion.

"Am I to be a laughingstock, defeated by *one* woman's vote?" Poseidon roared, and in his boundless rage, unleashed a storm that flooded the whole city, right up to the peak of the Acropolis. Hundreds were drowned.

It so happened that more men survived than women.

At the next assembly, therefore, men prevailed. And they decided:

"Poseidon punished us on account of our women. Therefore, from now on, women can't be citizens, can't vote, can't hold property, shall not even be allowed to pass their names on to their children. The previous vote for Athena doesn't count—"

"That is unjust," one woman spoke out.

"Be silent," men shouted. "Only we have the vote. And we say, Poseidon is our champion—"

Suddenly, right there inside the hall, a rainbow appeared. Iris, Zeus's messenger, stood in their midst and said, "Stop! Zeus has called the gods and goddesses together to decide this matter."

That ended the city's assembly.

Up on Olympus, Zeus, Ares, Apollo, Hermes, Dionysus, Hera, Hestia, Demeter, Artemis, and Aphrodite all convened in council—five gods, five goddesses. Poseidon and I could not participate, since we were the contenders.

Who voted for whom was never revealed. But as I imagine it, they voted by gender: goddesses for me, gods against me. Zeus abstained. That made the vote five in favor, four against.

I won.

I became the champion goddess of that city, from then on called Athens. It took its name from me. I defended it against its enemies. I gave it my best inventions. I helped it to flourish and grow.

In return, the citizens built me a temple atop the Acropolis, the greatest temple there had ever been. At the entrance stood my likeness, a thirty-foot-tall statue made of gold and ivory. And every year, in summer, on my birthday, the Athenians held a splendid festival, the *Panathenaea*, with gifts, athletic games, and a procession in my honor. And every fourth year the Athenian women (my aptest pupils at the loom) clothed my statue in a fine new *peplos* that they wove.

I helped the Athenians build seawalls and floodgates against future damage. And I decreed that the day on which Poseidon had loosed his dreadful flood on Athens be stricken from the calendar.

Iris is the rainbow goddess.

Dionysus (dy-o-NY-sus), son of Zeus and Semele (SEM-el-ee), is the god of wine and ecstasy.

Hestia (HES-tee-ah) is the goddess of hearth and home.

Artemis, daughter of Zeus and Leto, twin sister of Apollo, is goddess of the wilderness and hunting.

This temple is called the Parthenon (PARTH-en-ahn, parthenos means "virgin").

Peplos—a woman's embroidered robe, draped in folds, worn over other garments.

The other wrong remained. Women did not become citizens again. They led subjugated lives. Daughters were not taught to read or write. Fathers, without asking, chose husbands for them. And husbands ruled over wives, much as masters over slaves.

❖ I complained of this one day while strolling with my father in the garden of his golden dwelling on Olympus.

He shrugged it off, said, "Humans must be as they are and live as best they can."

"But, Father, *you* keep two jars beside your throne. The jars contain both good and bad, which *you* dole out to humans."

"True, but I don't brood about it. Why should I? Whatever befalls them, in the end they die. In a hundred years, or less, not one now living will still be alive." He tapped a finger to my forehead. "Pallas Athena, you think too much."

"No, Father—"

"And only you dare contradict me. Why?"

"On account of Metis. Her thought lives in me."

"And in me." The look in his eyes grew softer. "You're right. Think all you can. Just don't worry so much about humans. In a thousand years or less, they'll pray to other gods. But we'll live on, and thrive." He snapped his fingers, called for Hebe.

Hebe (HEE-bee), daughter of Zeus and Hera, was cupbearer to the gods and goddesses till Ganymede (GAN-ee-meed), a Trojan boy whom Zeus made a god, replaced her.

Hebe brought us cups and poured out nectar.

Zeus drank, and sighed contentedly.

I drank, and thought of humans, what they might be doing in a thousand years, or two, or three. I spun my thoughts into a shining, many-colored thread.

While I was thus occupied, Aphrodite paid a visit.

She and I were none too friendly even then, though it was long before the day when we'd become sworn enemies, vying for the golden apple that would start the famous Trojan War.

Zeus ran to greet her. He showered her with compliments. He plied her with nectar and eagerly asked, "Have you come to tell me of an enticing creature—nymph, or girl, or goddess—whom I might pursue?"

Aphrodite whispered in his ear.

Just then Hera entered.

Zeus squared his shoulders, innocently gazed her way, pretending that nothing could be farther from his thoughts than new illicit love entanglements.

Meantime my many-colored thread was spun. And I envisioned the design for a tapestry into which I'd weave my bravest deeds, most prized inventions, and my hope that humans, even in the farthest future, will remember me. . . .

APHRODITE

The wind gods knew it, and the seabirds knew it, the moment they caught sight of me: There never was, or is, or ever can be, anyone as beautiful as I.

Have you heard the poets sing my story?

Hear it from *my* lips:

Once upon a golden morning in the timeless long ago, Heaven threw his seed into the sea. It gathered foam. The sun shone down. The foam began to glow. It took form, *my* form—perfection. I, Aphrodite, was born.

Feet resting on a scallop shell, I surged to the top of a wave. All the waves around me crested and stood still. Gulls and sea hawks stopped their screeching. Wind gods held their breath.

Later on, as you shall hear, I would receive a golden girdle. Poets say it gives me magical allure.

The poet Homer describes the wondrous girdle in The Iliad.

Yes, it is a wondrous girdle. But the poets don't quite understand. Once every thousand years or so, I lend it to another—say, a goddess, girl, or woman. It gives *her* magical allure. *I* don't need it. I never needed it.

On that first bright morning, when I came into the world, the west-wind god fell headlong into love with me. He hugged my knees, he kissed my toes. The other wind gods were smitten, too.

I was naked, unadorned; no golden girdle then, only sea spray round my waist.

I am the goddess who ignites desire anytime, in anyone I choose.

✤ "Lovely Aphrodite, where may I carry you?" Zephyrus, the west-wind god, murmured in my ear.

"Someplace green and flowering," I said.

"Green? Flowering?" He did not understand.

"Somewhere sunny, then."

He swept me up. We wafted over the broad sea. He set me down on Cythera, a sunny island, oh but pale. The ground and trees were bare—and it was already April! ("Love's spring," a poet called that month. That poet understood me right.)

Cythera (SITH-er-ah) is an island to the south of the Peloponnese in the Sea of Crete.

That poet was Shakespeare.

Yes, I'm the goddess who brought spring. Wherever I trod on Cythera, fresh shoots of grass appeared, and daisies, myrtle, crocuses. Every bush my fingers touched burst into fragrant bloom. Every tree branch I could reach sprouted new green leaves.

And I'm the one who dreamed up love. Ask any river deity or ash-tree nymph or faun, What did they know of love before I came? Only haste and brutishness. Who taught them flirty glances, soulful whispers, gentle kisses, all those sweet refinements, if not I?

Nymphs are minor goddesses. They live in trees or rivers.

Fauns, also called satyrs (SAY-terz), are woodland gods who like to roughhouse and carouse. They have horns, pointed ears, goats' legs and hooves, and they enjoy chasing after nymphs.

✤ How long did my first golden morning last?

Nobody knows. There weren't any humans yet, and

they're the ones who count the passing years. I only know it wasn't noon yet when my wind god swept me up from Cythera and wafted me to fertile Cyprus.

Turtledoves flocked from the treetops, cooing—I understood them perfectly: "We're glad you've come! Great Aphrodite, let us serve you."

They fluttered around me, their feathers glistened in the sun. And I danced all over Cyprus, keeping company with naiads, dryads, satyrs, and such.

Often, when the winds came blowing, my turtledoves would lift me up, and I'd glide to the mainlands or to other islands, east and west. Everywhere I went, I did my work—or call it pleasure: I changed the lonely into lovers—regardless whether they were gods, goddesses, or mortals. (Yes, in case you've wondered, by that time there were humans on the earth.) And for sweet variety, I made sure these lovers change their partners now and then.

It's what I was born to do. Some praise, some blame me for it. To the blamers, I would say: Blame the sky for turning many different colors, blame the rain and snow for falling frequently.

Always after my excursions, I'd return to Cyprus, island of soft-sanded beaches, gently rolling hills, and sheltered valleys where I felt at home.

How long did I frolic there? A week, a year, or was it centuries?

✚ Meanwhile the reign of Titan god-king Cronos ended. Zeus became the new god of the world.

When Zeus's reign was well begun, he sent the Hours to summon me.

They are the goddesses who regulate the seasons (or else it would always be spring!). They see to it that summer comes, and autumn, winter, all in proper order. Another of their occupations is serving Hera as her maids. How she must have raged and ranted when she learned that they'd be serving *me*!

They clothed me in a fine white gown. They crowned me with a golden wreath, hung earrings from my earlobes, necklaces over my bosom, and they clasped the golden girdle round my waist.

"There, that's better," they said.

Better than perfection?

I thanked them. I loved the gown, the jewels, and that golden girdle with its exquisite filigree. But I had to laugh that these earnest goddesses did not understand this simple truth: Perfection is, well, perfect. Beauty such as mine can't be added to.

"Now you are suitably attired," the Hours' leader said. "Come, follow us." They stepped into the sky.

My doves clasped the hem and sleeves of my gown in their beaks, lifting me, and flew swiftly, smoothly, ever higher, past all clouds, up to the highest mountain peak, where Zeus's palace stands and eager gods awaited me.

✤ Entering the feasting hall, I took their breath away. All the gods jumped down off their couches and came running. Except for Zeus.

He sat motionless. Formerly he'd only sensed my presence. Now he *saw* me and was rapt. Slowly he descended from his high, bejeweled throne, stretched out his arms, and barred the others' way.

Hera, on *her* high throne, sent me a withering glance. Already then, although she'd never seen me, she knew of lovers I had led her husband to.

Her special bird, the peacock, perched above her, spread his gorgeous tail to its full expanse, as though to call attention to Hera's majesty.

Demeter, Persephone, and Leto smiled at me.

Athena, Hestia, and Artemis were stony-faced. To this day, they scorn my pleasures, choosing to stay virgins— why? Are they afraid that love brings pain? I pity them. They'll never know how readily love's joy blots out love's woe.

Zeus sent the gods back to their couches. He alone came forward, his sky-bright eyes intent on mine.

He'd been aware of me for ages—of course, how not? He knew me as the will that put desire in his heart.

He came nearer. But the peacock gave a piercing screech. Its meaning was as clear as if Hera had commanded, "Husband, stop!"

Zeus stood still. "Fairest goddess—" he began, but his voice grew thick. I could almost feel how much his fingers itched to touch my silken hair. But he did not dare. He cleared his throat, regained his composure, and resumed, "Aphrodite, I hereby adopt you. From this day forth I will be your father."

"*Adopt* me? Why?" I laughed; I often do at solemn moments. "I thank you, Zeus. It's kind of you. But I am not a child and do not need a father."

Zeus furrowed his brow. He thought his own thoughts. Then he confided, speaking just to me: "I have power over everybody. But in matters of the heart, you've

Demeter (de-MEET-er), goddess of fertility, is Zeus's and Hera's sister.

Persephone (pur-SEF-o-nee) is Demeter's and Zeus's daughter.

Leto (LEE-toh), once loved by Zeus, is the mother of Artemis and Apollo.

wielded power over me. And often. Aphrodite, you've been less than kind."

"How so?" I was surprised. "Didn't you appreciate the many loves I sent your way?"

"Yes. But some were mortal, and gave me mortal children. It makes me sad when I must watch them age and die."

Ah, now I understood his wanting to adopt me:

Daughters, even goddesses, are in their fathers' power. Zeus thought that as my father he could more readily control me, tame me, and make me find him only deathless goddesses to love.

Well, we'd see.

I accepted. "I will be your daughter."

"Good. You won't regret it. I'll give you a luxurious palace on whatever peak of Mount Olympus you like best. Shrines and temples down on earth, as many as you want. Festivals in your honor. Flowers, first fruits, sacrifices. Cyprus as your sacred island, a palace with a garden there, a tree with golden apples on it." This last he whispered, so that Hera wouldn't hear. "A splendid chariot—"

Hera has the one and only golden apple tree—so far.

"*I'll* make the chariot of finest gold!" The smith god Hephaestus stumbled to his feet. (He's lame, the only ugly god, with a squashed-in face, a scraggly beard, and misshapen body.) "I'll go at once and stoke the fire in my furnace." He looked at me with yearning, then limped toward the door.

Zeus invited me, "Now join our feast."

Hermes beckoned charmingly to me. I went and reclined on the couch next to his.

Hebe brought me a goblet and filled it with nectar.

Hermes, while whispering compliments to me, all of a sudden slid to the floor.

The war god, Ares, had sneaked up, pushed Hermes off the couch, and taken his place. Without a by-your-leave, he flung his arm around me. It was disrespectful. I meant to edge away. Instead I moved closer to him. Something about the way he grinned—so unabashed and so triumphant—set my spine to tingling, and I shivered, through and through.

Ares (AH-rayz) is a son of Zeus and Hera.

❖ Zeus's first "fatherly" act was to give me a husband—Hephaestus!

Everyone expected I'd object. But I was amused. I thought, "Ugliest husband, most beautiful wife—why not? We'll make an unusual pair!"

Besides, Hephaestus was a dear. He brought me presents every day: pretty mirrors, amulets, jeweled hair clasps, bracelets, rings. And he never failed to say, "Nothing can enhance your beauty," for which I gave him kisses, as many as he wanted.

Another good thing about this husband: His work kept him extremely busy. The gods and goddesses were always asking him for weapons, shields, and whatnots. He spent long hours at his furnace. This gave me ample time both for *my* work—making others fall in love—*and* for my recreation—amorous flirtations—or, in Hera's unkind words, adulterous affairs with other gods.

Hermes was one. I liked him for his air of mystery and prankishness, an intriguing combination. We had much sport, and an unusual child together: Hermaphroditus, son; no, daughter; no, really, son *and* daughter, and beautiful, and handsome, resembling us both.

I also reveled with the wine god Dionysus. By him, I had a son, Priapus (whom I love dearly, but, lest you be shocked, I would rather not describe his somewhat gross appearance).

Of all my many lovers, Ares was the roughest; never subtle, always more the soldier than the swain. And yet— I can't explain it—I found myself most often in his brawny arms.

I gave Ares lots of children. Of these, my favorite is Eros, the boy god with the bow and arrows. He's mischievous, self-willed at times, but mostly he obliges me and shoots his love shafts at whomever I decree.

Speaking of children, I pity goddesses who have none. Children give us pleasure—*if* they were fathered by a god. If not . . . ah well, that's different. Then there's a heavy price to pay, as Zeus knew and as I was to discover. But that came much, much later. . . .

As was bound to happen, Ares and I were spied upon, discovered in each other's arms. The sun god, Helios, that busybody, snitched on us, and our sport was over.

Hephaestus had been nurturing suspicions, but now he knew for sure and flew into a rage.

Ares suddenly remembered he had business to attend to in far-off Thrace. And he fled, leaving me alone to face the aftermath: everybody jeering, pointing fingers— as if what I'd done had never been done before!

Hera lectured, on and on, "Have you no morals? Do

Eros (EER-os) is best known in our time by his Roman name, Cupid.

Helios (HEE-lee-os) is both the sun and its god. He sees and hears everything that happens everywhere.

Thrace is a land northeast of Greece.

you deny that marriage partners should be faithful to each other?"

"As Zeus is faithful to you?" I wanted to say, but being in sufficient trouble, I held my tongue.

Of all the gods and goddesses, only Zeus was kind to me. He called the others hypocrites, reminded them of indiscretions *they'd* committed. And I thought, It's not so bad to have Zeus for my father.

✤ In gratitude, I found a new and perfect love for him. At least I *thought* she'd be perfect: silver-footed Thetis, whom everyone admired, a goddess of the sea, and guaranteed immortal.

Thetis (THEE-tiss).

She felt honored, she said. "Yes, let him come."

Zeus was pleased, and he thanked me. But it was not to be.

When he went down to the sea, Proteus came floating to the surface. He's the god they call "the old man of the sea," and he foretells the future, though in a lesser way than great Apollo, god of prophecy.

Proteus (PRO-tee-us) could take on many different shapes; hence the word pro-tean, meaning "variable."

Proteus told Zeus, "Beware. Don't go to Thetis. She's not meant for you."

"*You* beware. Don't spoil my pleasure," Zeus replied, annoyed.

"I must warn you," Proteus insisted, "if you make love to Thetis, she will bear a son—"

"Excellent. She is a goddess, he will be immortal, and I won't have to worry that he'll die."

"That is true. But he will be greater than his father,

and you know what that portends. As surely as my beard is green as seaweed, he will overthrow you."

Zeus grabbed hold of Proteus by that beard and shook him.

"Stop! Let go! It's not my fault, Zeus! I don't decree events, I just foretell them, and I'm hardly ever wrong."

Zeus had to heed the warning. He didn't go to Thetis, and he was very disappointed.

I was disappointed, too. I'd meant to do him a favor, that was all.

Only later would I realize what he must have thought: That I'd heard the prophecy. That I was scheming for his downfall and deliberately sent him to engender such a son. . . .

❖ A mortal, King Peleus of Thessaly, fell in love with Thetis. We goddesses and gods all liked him for the generous libations he poured and the sacrificial animals he slaughtered on our altars. And Zeus, still fond of the bride, arranged a lavish wedding feast for them.

Pelion (PE-lee-on) is a mountain in Peleus's kingdom.

It took place in a sunlit meadow on Mount Pelion. All we Olympians, and throngs of lesser deities, attended.

Pan, a son of Hermes, is the god of pastures. He has goat legs and horns on his head.

Apollo played his lyre; Pan, his pipes. Hebe poured the nectar; human girls poured wine. The Muses sang, the Graces danced; so did we all, with pleasure and abandon.

The three Graces, daughters of Zeus and Eurynome (u-RI-no-mee), are Aphrodite's handmaidens.

Only Eris, goddess of quarreling, was not invited.

The occasion was so festive, old dislikes were put aside. Athena and Hera chatted with me, as though we were good friends.

Eris (AYR-iss, "strife"), according to some sources, is the daughter of Nyx (niks, "Night"); others say she is the war god Ares's twin.

Suddenly the uninvited Eris put in her appearance, for once not looking grim, but festive, hair neatly combed, and smiling. She greeted us three goddesses by name. "I brought you something," she said sweetly.

She stooped down and rolled an object toward us.

It was round and shiny—a golden apple, with these words inscribed on it: "To the fairest."

I reached for it. So did Athena. So did Hera. We tussled, grappled, almost came to blows.

Peleus rushed over, stepped into our midst, lunged down, picked up the apple we'd let fall, ran to Zeus, and placed it in his hands.

Hera and Athena followed, shouting, "Husband, Father, give it to *me*, to *me*!"

I stood still, said nothing. I let my beauty speak for me and trusted Zeus to judge the matter right.

"No dispute shall spoil this happy feast," he said. He held the apple in the air and called, "My eagle, come!"

The giant bird swooped down, grasped the apple in his talons, and flew away with it.

"Unjust! Unfair! It's *mine*, it's *mine*," Hera and Athena clamored.

Zeus spoke soothingly to them. "Dear wife, dear daughter, understand me: As your husband, as your father, and also Aphrodite's father, I wish to please all three of you. But if I award the prize to one, I offend the other two. An impartial judge is needed. I will find one, be assured." He took their hands. He looked into their eyes. He begged them, "Don't be angry." And he never even glanced in *my* direction!

❖ I snapped my fingers in the air. At once my doves came flying, lifted me up, and whisked me off to Cyprus.

I strode into my garden, straight to my golden apple tree. It was laden with a hundred apples, each lustrous as the sun. And they all belonged to *me*!

Then why fret about that other apple?

Because it was my due!

Besides, I'd trusted Zeus. I'd started to feel fond of him, as daughters do of kindly fathers. I'd even hoped he would console me, ease my mourning for a lover whom I'd lost. Instead, my "father" had coldly slighted me!

Very well, I'd show him. I would make him sorry, and I knew just how.

I lay down on the soft ground, gazed at the gleaming fruit, and dreamed up love adventures, or rather *mis*adventures for my would-be father.

I made them all happen, and swiftly, too. I sent him from one lover into the next one's arms. They all were human women. They gave him human children who would age and be undone by their mortality.

Zeus grew angry with me. So be it, I thought. It didn't worry me.

❖ One afternoon he came to visit, seeming kind and well disposed. We strolled around my garden. He admired the golden apple tree. "How well it thrives," he said. And I thought, from the way he smiled, that he was sorry he'd withheld that other apple from me.

He spread his cloak out on the ground. We sat down in the shade. He pulled me close. "Daughter, we all miss you on Olympus. Don't you get lonely down here?"

I said, "I have the local deities, and fauns and such. They keep me company."

"What about lovers, if I may ask?" He gave me such a gentle look, then answered his own question. "Of course you have lovers. I just wonder, as your father—" He sounded so solicitous! "Has loving ever made you sad?"

He tilted my chin up, so fondly!

The sorrow I'd been feeling—oh, I wanted to confide it but was still not sure I should.

"You suffer even now, I see it in your eyes. Dear Aphrodite, trust me. Tell me."

He spoke so gently, gazed at me so tenderly, words started flowing from my lips, and I confided this whole story, of which I hadn't breathed a word to anyone:

"There was a woman who insulted me—here on Cyprus, where I'm used to being held in high regard. She boasted that her daughter was more beautiful than I. You can imagine how this made me feel. I punished her, and harshly: I drove the daughter mad with love for her own father.

"The daughter—Myrrha was her name—stole into her father's bed. She conceived a child by him, then could not live with what she'd done. She prayed to be changed into a tree.

"Some god, I don't know who, obliged her: Her feet took root. Her skin grew rough and hardened into bark. Just then, her pains came on, and she gave birth. She took the baby in her arms. Her arms grew stiff, turned into myrrh-tree branches. They held the baby too tightly, squeezing the breath from him.

"He was about to suffocate. Just then a boar came charging, sank his tusks into the branches, split them open, and the baby tumbled down.

Persephone (per-SEF-o-nee), the wife of Hades, is queen of the Underworld.

"I found him lying on the ground beside the tree. He gurgled; he was glad to be alive. I picked him up and dandled him, gave him the name Adonis. But, as you know, I don't much like taking care of babies. I've always let nymphs tend to my own offspring while they're small and tiresome.

"I put this tree-born baby in a basket and sent him to Persephone. She'd told me that she longed for one and said she'd send him back when he was bigger.

"Adonis grew tall, strong, handsome in her care, and she refused to part with him. 'I raised him, so he's mine,' she claimed. 'Finders, keepers,' I replied. 'And *I* found him.' We argued till we reached a compromise: Adonis was to spend one-third of every year with me; one-third with her; and the third portion with whom he pleased.

"It pleased him to spend it with me. It pleased me, too. He was still a boy, and liked to romp and run about, hide himself, jump out at me, rush away and challenge me to catch him. We made up games, we laughed, we teased, enjoyed ourselves the whole day through. I'd never known what I had missed, not having been a child myself. Adonis made it up to me: He taught me how to play.

"At dusk we'd lie down on a mossy bed and kiss. His lips were made for kissing all night long. And I gave him hints of pleasures we two would explore when he outgrew his boyhood.

"But he loved hunting. He grew tired of our games. Instead, he took up archery; shot at wild beasts for target practice.

"His fearlessness filled me with dread. 'Only shoot rabbits and hare,' I begged. 'Avoid the beasts with quills and tusks and claws. Adonis, my dearest, if any beast so much as scratches you, I'll feel it right here.' I placed his hand between my breasts and let him feel my heart beat loud.

"But the more dangerous the prey, the more he thrilled to stalk it.

" 'Avoid wild boars, especially,' I pleaded. 'One freed you from the tree's embrace and thrust you into life. Don't let another take your life away!'

"What I most feared came true. Another, wilder boar came crashing through the undergrowth. With cruel tusks he ripped through my beloved's chest. Crimson blood gushed from the wound. From the blood sprang crimson flowers—anemones, bright, fragile, lovely. Oh, what use were they to me? I'd have given all the flowers in the world to have Adonis back."

My story done, I sighed, and let my head sink onto Zeus's shoulder. "Now, Father, will you comfort me?"

"What for?" He shrugged me off. "We're used to humans dying, they do it every day. We only grieve when they're *our* children. *Then* we suffer—thanks to you. But you yourself have never suffered thus. You have no child by Adonis or by any other mortal lover."

He stood up, looked around. "Where's Eros, by the way? Ah, there, I see him."

My son was practicing his marksmanship, shooting arrows at a target on a tree.

Zeus nodded curtly to me and went to speak with Eros. Then he left.

At supper that evening, I asked my son what Zeus had said to him. The rascal wouldn't tell me.

✦ That night I dreamed—it seemed more real than waking—that I was wandering along the steep slopes of Ida, the many-footed mountain that stands above Troy. There I saw a godlike man. And a terrible longing clutched my heart.

I awoke, breathing "Anchises," a name I'd never heard, then cried out, "Aii!" Something stung my shoulder. A drop of *ichor* fell onto the bedsheet.

I paid it no mind. I hurried out of bed and over to my temple. I called to the Graces, "Come help me to prepare!"

"For what festival?" they asked. "What ceremony in your honor? When will it be held, and where?"

"In secret, far from here."

They bathed me in fragrant water and smoothed my body with heavenly oils. I put on a flame-colored robe, and brooches, earrings shaped like flowers, shining necklaces also. And I hastened through the cloudy night on desire's wings.

I came to Mount Ida. I ran through its forest. I'd never been there, yet I knew precisely where the pastures lay and in what forest clearing the herders' shelter stood.

Poets aptly call this mountain "mother of wild animals." Gray wolves and grim-eyed lions, bears, and leopards came toward me. But I was as wild as they that night. They sensed I did not fear them, and fawned and stroked me with their paws, as though asking to share what had brought me on this journey. So I put desire in their breasts. And they went off in pairs, to mate.

I hurried to the clearing.

The herders and their cattle were over in the grassy

Troy, the famous city, stands in the northwestern corner of Asia Minor on a height overlooking an inland waterway called the Hellespont.

Anchises (an-KY-seez).

Ichor (I-kor) is the immortal bloodlike liquid in the veins of goddesses and gods.

The lyre (lyr) is a musical instrument with strings to pluck. Hermes made the first one, using a tortoise shell.

pastures. One man alone, of princely bearing, stood outside the shelter. He played the lyre, high and clear, more thrillingly even than when great Apollo plays. I knew this man; I recognized him; I had dreamed him: He was Anchises, in the flesh.

When we appear to humans, if we don't wish to frighten them, we dwindle and diminish our radiance.

I did this. Yet he knew me for a goddess. "Let me build you an altar here on Mount Ida," he said, bowing low. "I'll bring you sacrifices—"

"No, Anchises, you're mistaken." I wanted him proud and manly, not shy or overawed. "I am an earthly girl, born of earthly parents. *Wealthy* parents," I added. And a pretty story flew into my head:

"Do you wonder how I came here? My friends and I were dancing in the woods, observing the rites of Artemis. A god came, Hermes on his winged sandals, and snatched me away, carried me off into the sky. 'You are to marry Anchises, the renowned descendant of Trojan kings,' he said. Oh, I was frightened. But now that I am with you, I'm filled with happiness. My parents will be happy, too, and proud to have you for their son-in-law. They'll send much gold, and woven stuffs, and many head of cattle as the bride gift."

"I'm happy, too. I'm overjoyed!" Anchises said, no longer afraid. "Since Hermes wills it, and it's destined we're to marry, no god or man can make us wait, or stand between us."

He took my hand. "Come, be my love." We went inside the shelter. There stood a couch spread with soft skins of bears and lions that he had slain. He loosened my girdle, he stripped off my gown.

We lay together. If this was Zeus's will, what of it? *I* willed it, too, with my entire being.

Anchises, in his manliness, erased my much-mourned boy Adonis from my mind.

He gave himself to me with such surrender, I thought, "He doesn't care if nothing's left of him when we are through. . . ." Then thinking ceased, as wave on wave of loving took me to a height where even I had never been before.

By morning, my terrible longing was stilled.

With daylight came reason. With reason came knowing:

It was *Zeus* who'd set me dreaming. *Zeus* had sent me here, and I now knew why: To repay me for all the times I'd thrust him into mortal women's arms. And of course I knew as well what had caused the stinging in my shoulder and the drop of *ichor* on my sheet. "Eros, while your mother's sleeping, shoot an arrow; let it graze her skin," Zeus had asked my son, and Eros had obeyed.

Furthermore, I knew that Zeus, this very morning, was telling all Olympus that he'd taught the love goddess a lesson; that he trusted I would send him on more fitting love adventures from that day on.

Finally, I knew that I would bear a mortal child.

I stood up from the fur-strewn couch. I towered above my lover and shone in my unearthly beauty.

"Anchises, wake up!"

He quaked and shook. "I knew you were a goddess—"

"You needn't be afraid. Promise me you won't reveal

what took place here in the night, and no harm will come to you."

I pushed aside the shaggy goatskins that hung in the entrance. "I will bear you a child," were my parting words to him.

I went outside. I made myself invisible and watched the herders return from the pasture, bringing goats' milk, loaves of bread. They sat down on the ground outside the shelter for their morning meal.

Anchises joined them.

I listened to them talking—about women, as men do. One said, "I'll wager that my sweetheart makes love better than your women can, and even Aphrodite—"

"Impossible!" Anchises blurted. "You're a fool, you don't know! *I* know. I lay with Aphrodite—"

My name had not yet left his lips when lightning tore the sky in two, and Zeus hurled down a thunderbolt. He's quick to punish mortals when they brag.

It was lucky that I hovered near. I threw my golden girdle in the path of the thunderbolt. It veered, it spared Anchises, struck the ground instead. Nonetheless, it shocked him so severely, he doubled over and could never stand upright again.

Seeing him so bent and crooked, as though he'd suddenly grown old, cured me of ever desiring him again.

❖ My own appearance changed: my belly grew round. And I wasn't eager to show myself on Mount Olympus.

But Zeus convoked a Council of the Gods—so-called, as though we goddesses were not included. Yet we are expected to attend.

Just as I'd feared, my figure drew attention.

"And who might the proud father be?" Hera asked me mock-politely. "Surely not a lowly human. Oh, I beg your pardon—" She covered her mouth, as though to cough, but instead she laughed maliciously.

Apollo interceded. He placed his hand on Hera's shoulder. "Stop," he said. "Like me, you can foretell the future. Close your eyes. What do you see?"

"A mewling child, born out of wedlock," Hera said.

"A noble leader of his people. The founder of a great new city, to replace the great and ancient city that will be destroyed," Apollo prophesied in ringing tones.

And Hera stopped taunting me.

✦ In due time my son was born. I named him Aeneas. If he became a leader, and founded a city, that would please me; I'd be proud. Meantime, he was just as weary-making as my other offspring were as infants. So I let the wood nymphs raise him.

Aeneas (e-NEE-us), "deserving of praise."

When the child was five years old, I brought him to Anchises. Anchises was delighted. "I'm stooped and bent, but I will raise him, gladly. May I tell him of his goddess-mother?"

I said yes, then went my way. And for all his childhood years, unmotherly though this may be, I seldom thought of him.

✦ But that wretched golden apple with that maddening inscription often plagued my mind. Maddening, too, was Zeus's negligence. After all this time, he had still not set the matter right.

I lay stretched out on my favorite Cyprus beach one day, trying not to brood about it, when a pair of winged feet poked through a cloud, and my one-time lover Hermes landed beside me.

"I come as Zeus's messenger," he said. "Good news, dear Aphrodite. Zeus has found a judge who will—"

"Award the golden apple to the fairest?"

"Yes," Hermes said.

"At last!" I made him whirl me round and round in circles on the sand. "Who'll be the judge?" I asked him breathlessly.

"Someone you will like."

"I hope so. And some*where* I will like?"

"On a mountain you know well: Mount Ida."

"Ah, yes." I sighed. "Will it be soon?"

"This very day."

"I must look my best!" I ran to get my finest gown, my brightest jewelry.

Hermes caught me, held me fast. "You look your best as you are now. You're ready. Come."

His right arm went around my waist. His feet sprang up. That set his winged sandals moving, and we were in the clouds.

The caduceus (kah-DOO-shus) is a magic wand.

I touched his staff, the *caduceus*. Hermes holds it in his left hand. It is the last thing dying mortals see when he's about to guide their souls down to the Underworld. I thought how dreadful it must be to have to die. And I exulted in the blue, cloud-dotted sky, in the undulating greenness of the earth below, in my own quick senses and the steady beating of my heart. I thought, Oh, what a blissful thing it is to be a deathless goddess winging toward Mount Ida!

❖ Soon, there we stood: I, and wise Athena, queenly Hera, all without a stitch of clothing on. And a mortal—a mere shepherd!—sat in comfort on a tree stump, drinking us in with his eyes.

His name was Paris. He was the appointed judge. He held the much-disputed golden apple in his hands.

He showed no fear. Perhaps he'd never heard that mortals can go blind on seeing even just one goddess in her splendor.

He looked and looked. He gazed his fill, deliberating which of us three was fairest.

He might as well have pondered which is wettest: stone, wood, or water? Which is highest: anthill, rock pile, or Olympus?

I thought I'd rebuke him for taking so long. But his hair was raven black, and a lock of it fell over his forehead, which was wonderfully smooth and high. His lips began to curl, as though he was about to smile. A small declivity—a dimple!—became apparent in his cheek and lent his face a boyish touch. Oh, and his eyes were green, and deep, and keen. I found that I had no objection to their lingering on me.

Hera and Athena, though, are not susceptible to handsome youths. They felt humiliated, I knew. Then why did they submit to this inspection? Not just because Zeus asked them to, but because they're vain. It is a failing we goddesses all share. But those two are far more vain than

I. How else could they delude themselves and think that they could win?

To better their chances, they motioned to the judge, "Come closer," and whispered to him, *sws, sws, sws* . . .

For shame! I couldn't hear their whispering, but I knew what they were up to: promising to make him rich, powerful, victorious, and wise.

Could I do less? "Come over *here*, my sweet!" I murmured.

He wore a coarsely woven cloak. He carried a crooked staff such as shepherds use. But his dignified, proud bearing hinted that he was of noble blood.

I pulled him nearer. I blew a little breath into his ear. He blushed. I whispered, "Handsome, worthy shepherd, judge me the fairest goddess, and you'll win the fairest woman in the world."

His smile grew wide. He offered me the golden apple. I took it blithely in my hands. I didn't know what bloodshed would ensue.

✤ My hunch about Paris proved right: He was no ordinary shepherd.

One day he left his sheep to graze and wandered down Mount Ida's slope into the city. Hecuba, the queen of Troy, stood at her palace window, from which she recognized the boy's face in the man's. With a mother's keen remembering she shouted, "That's my son"—one who as a baby had been left out on the mountain, because an oracle had warned his father, Priam, that the boy would be the ruin of the city.

I prepared to keep my promise and help Paris win the

Priam (PRY-um) was king of Troy.

fairest woman in the world. She was Helen, Leda's daughter. I'd known her since the day she'd hatched from an egg.

Yes, egg. Laugh, if you like. I did, at Zeus turned swan, waddling web-footed, flapping his wings, making unmelodious noises—all for Leda, then his love. She found him irresistible, she ruffled his snow-white feathers. And he made her pregnant, which explains the egg.

Helen grew up and married King Menelaus of Sparta. That she had a husband wasn't my concern.

Menelaus went traveling, as kings often do. While he was away from home, I arranged that Paris visit Sparta.

Love came over him and over Helen, both at once, the moment they saw each other. He took her on his ship, they sailed away. The rest, as humans say, is history:

Menelaus returned and was furious at finding Helen gone. He vowed he'd win her back. Hera and Athena were still furious with me and promised Menelaus they would help him.

He called on his brother, Agamemnon, high king over all of Greece, and on all the lesser kings of Grecian lands to help him win his Helen back. Soon a thousand ships set sail for Troy. And so began the cruelest war the world had ever known, in which not only men but even we immortal goddesses and gods would fight, and injure one another dreadfully.

Some sages and some poets claim that it was all *my* fault and never would have happened but for Paris stealing Helen, thanks to me.

To them I say:

Remember the Fates, who weave their will into the

The three Fates outrank even Zeus in deciding what must happen.

Hector (HEK-tor) was Hecuba's and Priam's best-loved son.

strands of mortal lives. They thrive on bloodshed, they love wars, and *they* decree when wars are to erupt.

Remember, too, that even Zeus must bend his will to what the Fates decree. Or else Troy would have won, because Zeus loved that city. Once it was called Dardania, after Dardanus, its founder. This Dardanus was Zeus's son. Zeus had loved him best of all his mortal children (at least till Heracles was born—no doubt Hera will tell you about *him*).

Speaking of one's mortal children, my son Aeneas grew up even handsomer and stronger than his father in his prime. Next to Hector, he was Troy's most honored, bravest fighter.

Of all my children, even Eros, whom I dote on (never mind that time he shot at me), I loved Aeneas best.

Therefore, naturally, Hera and Athena hated him.

These goddesses and gods fought alongside the Greeks: Hera and Athena, Hephaestus, Hermes, and Poseidon.

These fought for Troy: Apollo, Ares, Artemis, and I.

Zeus, although he favored Troy, remained aloof and did not fight, lest his vast strength throw history off its course, and thereby turn the Fates against him.

Perhaps I, too, should have refrained. I had no shield, no weapons, and no battle skills. But I stood staunchly by my son Aeneas, protecting him as best I could each time he hurled himself into a fight. When I failed, and he was harmed, I felt the hurt of it.

Athena, in her tall, plumed helmet, with the dreaded *aegis* strapped around her chest, fought relentlessly, as she was born to do. One time she thrust her spear so deeply into Ares's chest that he cried out louder than if nine, no, ten thousand men had bellowed all together.

She incited a favorite Greek of hers, Diomedes, against me. "Stab Aphrodite. Do it!" she commanded. Diomedes was pious. He thought it wrong to harm a goddess. "It's right, because *I* tell you to," Athena said. "Go on, you'll earn my gratitude."

I was holding Aeneas; he'd been wounded in the leg. Diomedes rushed at me. His spear point tore into my hand, almost pierced it through. Immortal *ichor* poured out from the gash, and with it all my strength. Another moment and I'd have let Aeneas fall. But Apollo was nearby and took him from me, just in time.

Immortals, when we're sorely injured, lose awareness, just as humans do. Next thing I knew, Iris, the rainbow goddess, held me to her bosom. Zeus had sent her down to rescue me. And my devoted Eros flew along.

Iris brought me to Mount Olympus. There I recovered, and my hand was healed.

The war raged on for ten long years. Troy fell, consumed by fire. The Fates had willed it so.

My beloved son Aeneas was the only Trojan leader who survived. He dashed into the city's sanctuary and wrested a strange object from the flames—a wooden statue, very ancient, of a child, a girl. . . . I glimpsed it only for an instant. . . . I thought of Athena, how she'd looked when she was little . . . and I wondered, did that statue have a name?

❖ Aeneas took Ascanius, his young son; hoisted Anchises, his old father, on his back; found the one ship the Greeks had overlooked when they had burned the Trojan fleet; and with the few good men remaining of

Diomedes (dy-o-MEE-deez), a great Greek warrior later wounded by Paris.

The Trojan War, in which ancient Greece defeated the city of Troy, is commonly believed to have raged during the mid-1200s B.C.

Ascanius's (as-KAY-nee-us) mother, Creusa (kray-oo-sah), died in Troy. Her ghost foretold that Aeneas and Ascanius would make their home in Italy.

the soldiers who had served under his command, he sailed away toward his destiny.

After long years of voyaging, he reached the western land called Italy. There he fulfilled all that Apollo had foretold, and made me the proudest mother any hero ever had.

But even glorious heroes grow old. It is their nature. And I learned the bitter truth of what Zeus had said to me: Watching helplessly as death claimed my Aeneas brought me the deepest suffering I had ever known.

Nothing can wholly relieve me of it. But the city that he founded gives me comfort, makes me proud.

Italians call it Roma.

Spell it backward, and it's *Amor*. The word puts joy and laughter in my heart. It's Latin. But the whole world understands it. It means love.

Aeneas's adventures are told excitingly and beautifully in The Aenead *by the Roman poet Virgil.*

HERA

Aphrodite, Aphrodite—I am *sick* of hearing poets sing her praise. "Violet-crowned, the golden, laughter-loving one . . ." How she sets their hearts a-twitter! And they call her "Queen of Love"—what folly.

If love is like a firefly that flits about and quickly fades, then let her be its queen.

If love is sacred, and endures, then it is *my* domain.

Of me, the sky queen, poets say behind my back, because they are afraid of me, that I am jealous, angry, vengeful. Yes, so I am, quite often, but with reason.

When they say I'm unforgiving, they are wrong.

If that were true, I'd fail at being who I am: goddess of marriage, ever faithful to a faithless husband.

If I had not learned to forgive, I'd curse my immortality. I'd wish to turn to dust the way that humans do.

✣ Imagine utter darkness, no space, no air to breathe. That's how it was inside the stomach of our father, Cronos. He had heard a prophecy: "A child of yours will overthrow you."

"Never!" He made his mouth gape open, dark and wide. Rhea, our mother, looked on in horror as Cronos gulped

The poets Hera means, Hesiod (HEE-see-od) and Homer, lived in the eighth century B.C. Their works are the richest sources of information about Greek goddesses and gods.

Rhea (RAY-ah) is the wife of Cronos, the Titan god-king.

us children down—Hestia first, then Hades, Demeter, Poseidon, and me, last.

Later, Rhea bore another child. But this time she outsmarted Cronos. She took a heavy stone, wrapped it in swaddling clothes, and handed it to Cronos, saying, "Here's your newest son."

He swallowed it. The heavy bundle landed on my shoulders, bending me, crushing me down.

The stone made Cronos sick. While he lay groaning on his bed, our mother fled with our newborn brother and hid him in a cave in Crete.

Crete (kreet), a large island midway between Greece and Egypt, was the center of a culture called Minoan, which flourished around 3000 B.C.

Luckily, the wisest goddess, Metis, came along. It was she who'd given our mother the idea of handing the stone to Cronos. So now she knew what ailed him. "I can cure you," Metis said. "Here, Cronos, drink this down." She offered him a potion.

He drank it, and he vomited the stone, then us. The last child swallowed came up first, and that was I.

Imagine our joy at breathing sweet, fresh air.

Cronos was exhausted. He fell asleep. While he lay snoring, our mother returned. "Children, my children!" She hugged us to her bosom. "You must flee," she urged my brothers and my sisters. "Quick, before Cronos wakes up." And she kissed them farewell.

But she kept on holding me because I was the youngest. "Hera, I will take you to a far-off land beside a mighty river. You'll be safe and happy there," she said, and winged away with me.

✤ Around the edges of the earth flows the wide, torrential river Oceanus. It holds the earth together. Its god,

Oceanus (oh-shee-AH-nus) is a Titan, and Tethys (TETH-iss) is a Titaness.

named Oceanus, too, is father of all other rivers, and Tethys, his mate, is their mother. They live in a pleasant land at the westernmost edge of the earth. It was there my mother brought me, and they took me in, became my foster parents.

In that distant, peaceful land, flowers bloom the year-round. Nectar flows in all the brooks. The sky is of a bluer blue than you have ever seen.

One noontime, though, when I was strolling through a meadow, suddenly the sky turned black as night. An icy wind swept through the trees. The branches creaked. Leaves fell. And something else came tumbling down— a small bird, a nestling. I caught it in my hands. "Cuckoo, cuckoo," the poor thing mewled, all shivery and cold.

I let it creep into the bosom of my tunic.

There it settled, soft and smooth. It felt so much a part of me that when the change began, I wasn't certain whether it, or I myself, was growing large. A loudness— thunder!—jarred my ears. The ground fell away from my feet. Something—someone—lifted me. Where was I? In whose power?

The day grew bright again as suddenly as it had darkened.

A god had hold of me.

I'd never seen his face, yet it was familiar. The flowing hair, the jutting-forward nose and chin were just like— whose? My own, I recognized when seeing myself in his eyes. His eyes were different, though: not brown like mine, but of a blue that made the brilliant sky seem pale.

"You're Zeus, the one our father didn't gulp!" I cried, I laughed, my heart beat wild and loud. "Appearing as a

cuckoo, you surprised me. But really, I have always known that someday you would find me, and—"

I stopped. My ordinary vision blurred. I closed my eyes and glimpsed the future. This happens to me now and then.

Zeus asked, "What do you see?"

"You, wresting power from our father Cronos—"

"Yes, I intend to. I'll be sky king. And you will be my queen." He clasped me tighter. "You have soul-beguiling, oxen eyes, and arms as white as alabaster. How beautiful you are. Hera, Hera—" His deep, rich voice made my name into a song. And he said, "I'll marry you. Here beside the river Oceanus will our wedding be."

Marry, wedding—strange new words, like music playing on an unknown instrument. I closed my eyes, and saw us on a future day, standing in this meadow, side by side, well-wishers all around. I put my hand over his heart, and felt our two hearts throbbing, beat for beat, as one.

Zeus said, "Hera, you and I belong to each other forever."

Forever *is*. It neither starts nor ends. I felt myself already his, and gave myself to him.

❖ Before we could wed, however, there came the long, hard war with Cronos and his Titans. We sisters and brothers, and many other deities, fought on Zeus's side.

When we had vanquished all the Titans except Cronos, our brother Hades put his iron helmet on. Darkness seeped from its wide brim and rendered him invisible. On tiptoe, making not a sound, he stole into the armory

Most Titans, but not all, helped Cronos fight Zeus. The females, Titanesses, did not take part in that war.

where our father kept his weapons and took away each sword, shield, dagger, javelin, and bow and arrow Cronos owned.

Early next morning, our brother Poseidon entered the mountain cave where Cronos slept. Zeus followed stealthily, and I with him. I loved him so much already then, I never left his side.

"Cronos, slug-a-bed, awake!" Poseidon shouted.

Cronos started up, and groped around beside the bed. "Where are my sword and shield?" Not there. Hades had stolen these, too.

Poseidon jabbed at Cronos with the three-pronged trident. Cronos, weaponless, drew his knees up to his chest and cringed.

"Now!" I whispered, handing Zeus the strongest of all thunderbolts the Cyclopes, our allies, had been forging.

Zeus hurled it. Cronos hurtled off the bed. The cave began to crumble.

The Cyclopes (sy-KLO-peez) are one-eyed giants. Hesiod says they are Titans, but fought on Zeus's side. Homer says they are Poseidon's sons.

We dragged him out. He howled, he cursed us, then he wheedled, "Take pity on your father!"

"You took no pity on us children when you gulped us down," we said. And we bound him securely with chains.

Zeus exiled him to darkest Tartarus, which is as deep below the earth as heaven is above. The other Titans who had fought for Cronos were already there. And there they languish, imprisoned to this day.

✣ Zeus said, "Now that I have won, I must find the stone that Cronos swallowed."

"What for?" I asked.

"You'll see."

I went with him to the cave where our father had spewed it out.

We washed the stone clean and carried it to Delphi. There he set it down, at the foot of Mount Parnassus. "May this stone stand here forever." He touched his lips to it, and prayed, "Stone, remind me of my father's cruelty. Make me a better god-king, wiser and more just."

Delphi (DEL-fy), the mountain site believed by the ancient Greeks to be the midpoint, or the "navel," of the earth.

✦ Then Zeus divided up the world, alloting the sky and lands to himself; granting the sea to Poseidon; the Underworld to Hades. He built palatial dwellings on Mount Olympus for himself and me, for Demeter, for Hestia; and palaces down in their realms for Hades and Poseidon.

Later, Zeus built palaces on Mount Olympus for gods and goddesses of the next generation: Ares, Hephaestus, Apollo, Artemis, Athena, Dionysus, Hermes.

When that was done, he said, "I still have many matters to arrange to set the world in order. Dear Hera, you go home. Prepare for our wedding. We'll be together soon."

How long was "soon"? A dozen years? A century? Immortals don't keep track of time as carefully as humans do.

But immortals like to gossip, as much as humans do.

However long we were apart, Zeus was seldom alone. I learned this from Hermes, our chief carrier of tales. He told me about goddesses, girls, and women he had seen in Zeus's company; and went into great detail about this one's violet eyes, that one's shapely ankles, and still another's rosy cheeks and slender waist.

Naturally I felt jealous, who would not?

"Never mind. It's Aphrodite's doing," Hermes said. "She makes everybody misbehave. Even Zeus cannot resist her whims."

"Well, *I* resist. And Zeus will, too. Once we are married, he'll love only me," I said.

"To be sure," said Hermes, smiling. "And poets, if they mention Zeus's infidelities, will speak tactfully and say he entered into 'previous marriages.'"

"'Previous marriages?' What nonsense!" Little did I know how I much I'd learn to loathe that phrase. "Our marriage, his and mine, will be the first one ever. I believe in speaking truth. Let poets say, 'Zeus had his *flings*,' not beat about the bush."

✦ I thank whatever power decreed that we Olympian goddesses don't age. If not for that, I would have been a crone, toothless and wrinkled, hobbling to the altar when at last the sun rose on our wedding day.

But oh, you should have seen me! I was young as morning. I was lovely as the almond and acacia sprigs that my handmaidens, the Hours, brought to me.

They braided my bridal garland. They pleated my gown and helped me put it on.

These three young goddesses are Zeus's daughters from one of his countless "previous marriages"—to Themis, known for being proper! I'd often wondered: Where was *her* propriety, when she'd let Zeus make love to her? But on this day, I banished all such brooding from my mind.

Themis (THEM-iss, "order").

The Hours dressed and readied me for the festivities.

With Tethys to my right, and Oceanus to my left, I led the marriage procession through the flowering meadow down to the river where the altar stood.

Behind us danced the Graces, three. The nine Muses

Gamelion (ga-MAY-lee-on) was an early spring month in ancient Greece. In Roman times, when Hera's name became Juno, June became the wedding month.

followed, playing flutes and lyres. All these twelve young goddesses are Zeus's daughters from still other so-called previous marriages.

Done is done, is past, I thought. All that mattered was this flower-scented, shining day in the month hereafter called Gamelion, meaning "Wedding Month."

Zeus strode down from the sky. Everybody looked at him. He only looked at me.

No one could preside over this most sacred wedding. For who had more authority than Zeus, the highest god, and I, the highest goddess, now that he had chosen me?

As the sun's own fire blazed down on the altar, we ourselves performed the ceremony thus:

Zeus gave me a crown, a ring, and a scepter with a golden cuckoo, wonderfully lifelike, at the top.

I touched the cuckoo to my breast, honoring the form in which Zeus first appeared to me.

I spoke my vow: "I'll love you more each day."

I gave him an acacia blossom from my bridal garland.

He touched it to his lips. "And *I* will love *you* more and more, through all eternity."

"Now I am yours and you are mine forever," we said in unison.

Then, not a bird or cricket chirped. No breezes stirred. The guests sat hushed. In that perfect stillness I could almost hear the rustle of my girlhood slipping from me like a worn-out gown.

Zeus lifted my veil. We kissed. Now, as Zeus's wife and queen, I felt myself becoming a new goddess, long-awaited: marriage goddess, champion of devoted, faithful spouses.

The Graces showered us with blossoms, and the feast began.

✦ All the guests but one had brought us gifts: tripods, bedding, bowls, and other household things.

Only Gaia, oldest goddess, came with empty hands. She is the mother of the Titans, whom Zeus and we defeated. Resenting their imprisonment, she might well have preferred to stay away. I bowed to her and said, "Your presence in our midst is gift enough."

"Thank you for your gracious words. Come, show me your dear foster parents' orchard."

I led her there.

We walked past fragrant fruit trees, up a hill. From the top we could see the Atlas Mountains in the east and the river Oceanus flowing in the west.

Gaia stooped down. She stroked the ground, inscribing circles upon circles, murmuring a spell.

The ground cracked open.

A tree sprang up, ablaze with fruit.

We goddesses are used to radiance—our own, and other deities'. Even so, the sight of all those golden sun-bright apples—many hundreds!—dazzled me.

Gaia touched my forehead with the finger that had stroked the ground, and said, "This tree is my gift to *you*."

"To me alone?"

She nodded.

"Are you aggrieved with Zeus?"

She turned her face away, looked to the east, and called, "Daughters of Atlas, Hesperides, come!"

Seven nymphs came flying.

Tripod (TRY-pahd): a three-legged stand, used as a table or a stool, or to support a lamp or cooking vessel.

Gaia (GAY-yah, "Earth") was one of five first beings born from primeval Chaos (KAY-oss). The others were Tartarus ("Underworld"), Nyx ("Night"), Erebus ("Darkness"), and Eros ("Love's generating force," not yet personified).

These mountains are named after Atlas, the Titan who holds the sky up on his shoulders. In actuality, the Atlas Mountains are in Morocco, in North Africa.

The Hesperides (hes-PER-i-deez, "daughters of evening") are offspring of Atlas and Hesperis, a little-known goddess of evening.

"Hesperides, I order you to guard this tree. Let none but Hera pluck its fruit."

Even as these nymphs were promising that they'd keep watch, I glimpsed the future. For one fleeting, devastating moment I saw a thief—none other than my husband, Zeus—approach the tree.

The day would come when he would make the nymphs, all seven, look the other way. He'd pluck an apple, take a seed, grow a second tree—to give to Aphrodite. And she would brag about it just to spite and humble me. . . .

✤ After our wedding feast, my foster father Oceanus gave us a chariot with four swift horses harnessed to it, and we departed, driving swiftly through the sky.

When the sun sank low, we halted over Samos, island of my birth.

Samos (SAH-mos) is a fertile island in the Aegean Sea, close to the coast of Asia Minor.

"Clouds, make us a bower," Zeus commanded.

The clouds obeyed. They joined together, formed a fleecy chamber. The moon and stars shone through the walls, illuminating our wedding night.

Historians and sages say that Zeus had asked the sun god Helios not to rise, and not to drive his steeds across the sky, but to let the night continue for three hundred years.

Maybe so. I didn't count how many hours, years, or centuries it lasted. I only know it passed too quickly by.

✤ The next morning, as Zeus and I went strolling arm-in-arm through Samos, I thought about what my foster mother Tethys said when she helped prepare me for marriage: "Certainly the wedding night will give more pleasure to the bridegroom than the bride." But I had found such happiness, I wondered whether she was right.

Zeus said, "*I'd* always thought the bridegroom would. This morning, though . . . well, I'm not certain." He smiled at me, as though we two now shared a precious mystery.

Just then, by sheer coincidence, Tiresias came along—the only person in the world who could resolve our question.

This famous seer once—no, twice!—had had a strange adventure: He'd come upon two snakes entwined in coupling; he'd struck the female with a stick, whereupon he was transformed into a woman.

Seven years went by. Tiresias, now a she, saw another pair of snakes, or possibly the same pair, coupling. This time she struck the male snake; thereupon, she, Tiresias, became a man again.

"Well met, Tiresias," said Zeus, and asked him, "Tell us, who has greater pleasure from the wedding night: the bridegroom or the bride?"

"I cannot speak for deities," Tiresias replied. "With humans it is thus: A woman's pleasure in making love is nine times greater than a man's. This much I know because I have been both."

✤ What humans call "honeymoon" lasts but a month at most. Mine and Zeus's, I believed, was part of our "forever."

✤ I gave much thought to what Tiresias had said. I wondered: Do gods, do men, and did *my* Zeus have so many

Tiresias (ty-REE-see-us), a wise and very old Theban, reached the age of seven hundred! Among his ancestors was a soldier who sprang up from the dragon's teeth that Cadmus planted.

Eurynome (yoo-RIN-o-mee) is the mother of the Graces.

Europa (yoo-RO-pah), the princess whom Zeus—disguised as a bull—abducted, gave him three sons: Minos (MY-nos), Rhadamanthys (rah-dah-MANTH-iss), and Sarpedon (SAR-pe-don).

Leda (LEE-dah), to whom Zeus came as a swan, was the mother of Helen of Troy.

flings because they hope that numbers and variety will compensate for *our* sex having greater pleasure?

If this was so, I pitied them. I basked in newfound sweet contentment with my Zeus, and I pitied his "previous" lovers, too. I thought, He'll never come to them again! How sad they must be feeling: Metis, Themis, Eurynome, my own sister Demeter, Europa, Leda, on and on. The list was very long.

I was too happy to bear grudges. I wanted to extend a friendly hand to them, especially to Metis. After all, I owed her thanks for having helped our mother free us from our father's belly long ago. But I couldn't find her. She'd been absent from Olympian feasts and councils. No one knew where she might be.

I asked Zeus, "Have you seen Metis anywhere?"

He made an ugly face and said, "Don't speak of her."

"Why not? Did she displease you?"

"Be still, I beg you, do not speak at all—"

"Dear husband, what's the matter?"

"My head hurts." He threw himself onto our bed and closed his eyes. I pulled the window hangings shut, I fetched him a cool compress. It did not help. I felt such pity, it almost caused *my* head to hurt.

Metis will know a cure, I thought, and went to look for her.

One day, while I searched for her along the river Triton, I saw my husband, sitting on a boulder, clutching his poor head.

"It throbs!" he cried. "It wants to burst! Someone, anybody, help!" He screamed so loud, they heard him on Olympus.

Everyone came rushing down. Hephaestus, our firstborn, brought his hammer. "Use it," Zeus commanded, "strike me hard, right here!"

Hephaestus struck him, hard. Zeus's forehead opened and—wondrous sight!—out jumped Athena, fully armed, a little warrior goddess, shouting out delightedly at being in the world.

"Well done, Zeus!" The gods all clapped him on the back, congratulated him, and boasted, "A god, a male, brought forth a child! What a triumph for us all! Now there is nothing we can't do!"

We goddesses gave our congratulations, but with restraint. Bearing children, after all, had been our gender's one great glory in gods' eyes. Was this now lost? If so, by whose fault?

They all pointed at me.

Hestia said, "Hera, you're his wife, *you* should have borne the child. Were you afraid it would be ugly, like Hephaestus?"

Demeter asked, "Were you so vain, you wanted to stay slim?"

"You'll hate the little warrior goddess for cheating you of motherhood," said Themis.

They clucked their tongues, so smug, so know-it-all. I turned away. More troubling matters occupied my mind.

Hephaestus stood between me and the sun, casting a dark shadow over me. I thought, How big he's grown, and burly, this child of mine and Zeus's, begotten on our wedding night. . . .

I glanced from him to Athena, sprung from Zeus's head. Athena sat by the river, throwing pebbles in.

This question sprang into my mind: Just *how* did Zeus beget this child? By himself upon himself? A bitter laugh rose to my lips. No, *I* could not believe that.

Athena was little, still a child. . . . Just *when* did he beget her? . . . Not so very long ago. . . . But Zeus and I'd been married, oh, for many, many years. . . .

I struck my forehead with my fist. I'd trusted him. I'd thought that he was true to me, and done with all his "previous" flings—not so! Oh, what a fool I'd been!

Just when I felt most angry with myself, and most despondent, Athena offered me her little hands, cupped, filled with river water.

I sipped. She smiled at me. I took her on my lap, and instantly into my heart.

Despite what Themis had predicted, I would never hate Athena. On the contrary!

She kept on smiling. Her eyes were childish, big and round. But something deep and wise in them told of another parent, not Zeus alone, from whom she'd sprung.

Of course. There had to be a mother. That is a law no god, not even Zeus, can circumvent.

"Metis is my mother," Athena said, answering my silent thoughts. And suddenly I knew the rest:

There'd been a prophecy. There always is. An oracle had warned Zeus: "If Metis bears you a son, he'll overthrow you."

It's usually the future that I glimpse. But now, in a trancelike moment, the past revealed itself to me:

"Never!" I heard Zeus protest; I saw his mouth gape open, just like my father's mouth when he'd devoured me. The dreaded darkness I once knew swirled before my eyes again. A crushing weight bore down on me: not a swaddled stone this time, but the knowledge of what Zeus had done, despite his prayer to be a better god-king than Cronos.

"Zeus swallowed Metis down," Athena said calmly. "Metis lives inside him, and tries to give him wisdom—"

The horror of it made me gasp for breath.

✤ That night, alone with Zeus, I told him what I knew.

"It's no concern of yours," he said, and tried to take me in his arms.

Oh yes, it concerned me, it consumed me.

I tore my hair. I beat my breast. I loved him not a jot the less. I'd miss him badly. But his look of "*I'm* supreme, and *I* can do no wrong" so anguished me, I had to leave Olympus for a while.

✤ When Aphrodite wants to travel, she harnesses her frilly doves, they pull her golden chariot, and everyone applauds the pretty spectacle.

I can hitch my gorgeous peacocks to my chariot anytime I want, and enable them to fly. But I was in no mood for showing off. I wrapped a thick, black cloud around me, and willed myself back to my childhood home.

I landed in the orchard, beside my golden apple tree. I sank to my knees. I didn't know that I would pray, but these words burst from my lips: "Gaia, great mother, grant that I may bear an offspring on my own, apart from Zeus, and thereby find relief."

I touched my forehead to the ground. The ground was moist, it smelled of life, and all but answered, "You shall have your wish," so keenly did I feel the burgeoning in me.

✤ I stayed on earth for all the months in which my waist expanded. I visited my temples and let my women worshipers, especially those pregnant, bathe me, soothe me, tend to all my needs.

I was at Delphi on the day the creature in my womb began to twist and turn, impatient to emerge. Don't think we goddesses don't suffer birthing pains. I labored unattended, unrelieved, the whole day through.

Your every hair would have stood on end if you had seen the monster I brought forth—part scaly snake, part spiky dragon, fire flaming from his nostrils, stench seeping from his mouth.

Typhaon (TY-fah-on).

I called him Typhaon, a name most apt because it is the ancient word for smoke combined with putrid winds and hurricanes.

I knew of a chasm, hewn into the Delphic rocks, where an ancient priestess dwelled: Pythia, part crone, part serpent-dragoness—what better keeper for my monster?

Pythia (PITH-ee-ah) is the prophetess through whom the earth's most ancient oracle at Delphi speaks.

I brought him there.

She welcomed us. She dandled little Typhaon; she taught him how to flick his tongue. She had been longing for just such a darling creature to keep her company.

"He's yours," I said. But first I put him to my breast. "Suck, little Typhaon."

He did, with eager, smacking noises. I was glad. I felt as though the hideous creature I had spawned was draining wrath and bitterness out of my being, into his.

While nursing him, I closed my eyes and glimpsed this

Leto (LEE-toh) is the daughter of the Titan and Titaness Coeus (KO-ee-us) and Phoebe (FEE-bee).

woodland scene one future sunny spring: two little birds, a pair of quail, nodding heads, dancing their courtship— oh, cleverly disguised. But I recognized them. The cock was Zeus, the hen was Leto. I knew in a flash, she'd bear him twins: Artemis and Apollo. And they'd be greater deities, more splendid than any children *I* would bear. It was destined. Nothing could prevent it.

Ah, but little Typhaon would have grown tremendous by then. Sputtering and gurgling now, in that future he would bellow, he would roar. And I would ask him, as a favor, "Follow Leto, persecute her, blow your fetid breath on her, drive her on from place to place, make her pregnancy a torment, never let her rest. . . ."

Meantime little Typhaon emptied both my breasts. "Someday I'll come back for you," I said, and gave him into Pythia's care.

Argos, a major city in the Peloponnese, near the eastern shore.

✤ On my journey home I stopped near Argos. Weary and disheveled, I bathed in the river Canathus. I floated on its surface, hoping to rest. Instead, anxieties beset me: I'd left Zeus with no farewell. How would I explain to him why I stayed away so long? Had he taken my absence for betrayal?

When I swam back to shore I heard a young girl tell her friend, "People say this river can restore a woman's beauty in her lover's eyes."

"I believe it," her friend said.

Was this true? And could the river work its magic on me, a goddess, as well?

I hoped so, yet I doubted it as I emerged from the water, and anxiously returned to Mount Olympus.

✤ Zeus flung our palace portals open and swept me into his arms. He asked me not one question. "Embracing you is wonderful," he said. "It's like the first time in the meadow by the river Oceanus, only sweeter."

The power of *marriage* made this happen. Marriage is mightier than any river magic, and mightier than even I, its goddess, knew. It can restore itself, be whole again, even when betrayals have gnawed away at it.

✤ Speaking of rivers reminds me of Inachus. . . .

And speaking of betrayal, I must tell you about one so shameless, it makes my cheeks still burn.

Inachus (in-AH-kus), a river near Argos.

The river god Inachus had a daughter, Io. She was a very pretty nymph, with soft, brown, calflike eyes. Just right for Zeus, she'll please him, Aphrodite must have thought. And Hera will be furious—perfect!

Io (EYE-o).

Zeus saw Io and "was more smitten than he'd ever been before," so Hermes, the gossip, reported.

But Io was skittish. She ran from Zeus, though not too fast or very far. He caught her and tumbled her down in a shady grove of poplar trees.

What made this betrayal so much more outrageous than his others? Io was *my* priestess. That shady grove of poplars was on *my* temple's grounds.

Their pleasure was brief. Zeus saw me come storming toward them. He wanted to gather a fog around their lovemaking, but he couldn't, for the weather was too fair. Instead, he grasped her linen gown, meaning to change it into a cow's hide with which to cover her.

With some help from me, he failed in his intent. My

intent prevailed: Not only did the gown become a young cow's hide, all smooth and white, but Io's eyes grew larger, more wide apart; her arms became legs; her feet became hooves; her body lengthened, thickened; and from her round, white rear a stringy tail hung down.

"Now Zeus will want her less," I thought.

"May I be changed into a bull," I heard him mutter. He'd worked that transformation once before, when he'd stolen Europa and had swum across the sea with her.

"Oh no, you don't!" I stopped him, and demanded, "Hand over your beloved. It's only right. She was my priestess; now let her be my cow."

He agreed, reluctantly. He still desired her.

Io mooed. She was unhappy, and even more so when I sent a gadfly to keep her on the run.

As further precaution, I went to Argus, Io's brother, an oversized, odd-looking fellow, and a devoted worshiper of mine. I asked him as a favor, "Don't let Zeus come near your sister. Keep an eye on her."

Argus had a nickname, Panoptes (pan-op-teez), meaning "all eyes."

"Just *one* eye?" The oddity about this Argus was, he had one hundred eyes—in front, in back, all over him. "I'll watch her with all hundred eyes, both day and night," he promised.

Io ran to Inachus. "Father, help!" she tried to beg, but she could only moo, and moo. Inachus had no way of knowing that this miserable cow was a relative of his, much less his daughter.

Poor Io, what was she to do?

She raised one leg. She teetered on the other three and used her hoof to write the letters *I*, then *O* in the sandy riverbank. Luckily her name was short, for writing isn't easy when you have no hands.

Inachus read the writing in the sand. "Io! Oh, my dear!" He kissed her on her muzzle. He stroked her furry cheeks. He wept a flood of river tears because he lacked the might to make her be a river nymph again.

Argus came after her and took her by the halter.

Inachus pleaded, "Let her stay the night with me."

"No." Argus led her to a paddock. He locked her in, as he would do every evening, and watched her all night long.

But every power in the world has its opposing power. As Argus had a hundred eyes, so Hermes had his snake-encircled wand called the *caduceus*.

Hermes is a many-sided god: serious when guiding souls down to the Underworld; musical (he plays the lyre—invented it, in fact); salacious when he tattles tales; duplicitous when stealing cattle or protecting thieves. I, for one, don't like him much. He's one of Zeus's sons, but not by me.

I saw those two together, Zeus and Hermes, strolling through the clouds. I had a hunch Zeus was confiding how much he loathed Argus. And maybe he suggested, "What if some accident befell him. . . . Hermes, do you catch my meaning?"

By that evening, Hermes had befriended Argus and won the cowherd's trust. They sat together in the paddock. Hermes sang songs; he played the lyre.

"How soothing. I feel so lazy." Argus leaned against the paddock fence. He yawned; he rubbed a few of his eyes. "Say, by the way, what is that wand you're holding?"

Hermes's mother is Maia (MAH-yah), a daughter of Atlas and of the sea nymph Pleione (PLAY-o-nee).

"That is my *caduceus*." Hermes waved it, oh so innocently.

The *caduceus* can make whomever Hermes designates fall into a deep, mind-numbing sleep.

Hermes waved the wand till Argus, all eyes closed, lay stretched out, snoring loudly. Then, with a single dagger stroke, he sliced Argus's head clean from his shoulders.

That's why they call Hermes "Argus slayer."

✦ And why do peacocks' feathers have so many blue-green eyes?

When I discovered Argus dead, I retrieved his hundred glazed, dull eyes. I made them shine again. I sewed them to my favorite peacock's feathers. And he bequeathed them to all future generations of his male descendants.

✦ Poor Io. Now she mourned her brother, which made her mooing even sadder than before.

Zeus appealed to me, "Have pity on her."

"Why don't you change her back?" I asked.

"I can't—"

Can't? I'd never heard him say that word before.

"You know there is a law among us," Zeus continued: "No immortal, even I, can undo what another of us did. It was you who changed her. Only you can change her back. Dear wife, do this one thing for me." He asked me with such feeling that I could not refuse.

The Nile is a mythical and actual river in Egypt.

I called for my chariot. I drove to the Nile. That far had Io run and swum, with the gadfly goading her. In that river Io stood, staring down as though she wished to drown.

Surprised, she heard two splashes, and saw her horns

fall in. They sank to the bottom. She couldn't believe it.

She raised a foreleg, found she could touch her head with

it. Her head was smooth, no horns now! That foreleg was

an arm again, complete with hand—the other foreleg,

too. The hind legs lost their hooves, they sprouted dainty

feet, on which she stood upright, a pretty nymph with

milky white complexion, and she shouted, "I'm not moo-

ing, I speak words, oh joy! I'm Io, my own self!"

❖ "Io is a nymph again," I said when I came home.

Zeus thanked me from his heart, and promised: "I will

never take another lover. I'll stay with you, I won't deceive

you anymore, I swear it. I'll even solemnize this oath by

pouring a libation of water from the sacred river Styx that

leads down to the Underworld."

Whoever thus invokes the Styx, then breaks his oath,

must sink into a deathlike stupor from which he won't

awaken for a long, long while, and on awakening, is ban-

ished from Olympus for still longer.

"Bring me a cup of Stygian water," Zeus called to the

rainbow goddess, Iris. She has charge of it.

She came, but I waved her away. "No need to swear

by Styx," I said to Zeus, "your word is oath enough."

❖ In less than a week, he left. He went to Thebes. There

lived a woman named Alcmene. She was said to be

exceptionally brave, intelligent, in every way outstand-

ing—and beautiful. If not, would Zeus have sought

her out?

Zeus took the form of her husband, who was away at

the time. And he came to that woman in the night.

Thebes, the prominent city in central Greece where Cadmus planted the dragon's teeth.

Alcmene (alk-MAY-nay).

Heracles (HEE-rah-kleez).

Nemea (NEM-ee-ah), a city in the northern Peloponnesus.

Selene (se-LEE-nee), goddess of the moon.

As it happened, the husband returned unexpectedly that same night, soon after Zeus had paid his visit.

In nine months' time Alcmene gave birth—to twins. Alcmene's husband fathered one. My husband fathered the other, and they named him *Heracles.* I took it for a cruel joke on me.

Of all Zeus's betrayals, this one, whereby he broke his oath, hurt and enraged me most.

I set out for Thebes. On the way, I caught two serpents, deadly poisonous, but pretty, with shining scales of azure blue and little rattles in their tails. A baby might well want to play with them.

I put them in the crib with little Heracles. He reached right out and strangled them. He was that strong, even then.

He grew up ever stronger, and exceptional in every way: kind, polite, and daring, always eager for adventure, ready to set wrongs to right. He was everybody's favorite hero, just not mine.

No doubt you've heard of his adventures. Storytellers love to tell tales of Heracles. But none reveal the purpose he was born to carry out—a secret purpose of enormous consequence. Only Zeus knew what it was.

When Zeus returned to me from Thebes, we were together, yet divided. I was angry; he was gloomy. We hardly spoke. He made no mention of his newest son.

When Heracles slew the Nemean lion, who'd been suckled by Selene and was said to be invincible, I asked Zeus, "Aren't you proud?"

He nodded grudgingly, embarrassed.

When Heracles killed the notorious Cycnus, then cleared the sea of pirates, I asked Zeus, "Why must that son of yours perform so many labors and undergo so many trials?"

"To prove that he's a hero."

"Hasn't he already done so, many times?"

"Yes, but it's not enough." Zeus scowled. "Leave me alone."

Fine. And if more trials for Heracles were needed, I'd supply them willingly!

I unleashed the dog-bodied Hydra on him, a terrifying creature from a fetid, murky swamp. She had countless horrid heads, more than mongrel packs have fleas. Every time one head was severed from its slimy neck, a new head popped up, or two, or three. And tucked inside her cheeks were sacks of lethal venom.

Heracles cut, he slashed, he ducked, barely escaping her multiple menacing mouths. The Hydra's victory seemed assured. Even so, just for good measure, I sent along a crab of mammoth size to grasp him in its murderous pincer claws.

You'd think that fighting two such monsters at the same time would have been too much for any hero. Not for Heracles. He won, he killed them, only to contend with countless other foes I sent and obstacles I put into his way.

✦ Embittered, sick at heart, I'd chosen a small room in our palace for myself and avoided the spacious bedchamber I'd formerly shared with Zeus.

Cycnus (SIK-nus), a son of Ares. He put skulls on the road to trip up travelers, then robbed and murdered them.

The Hydra (HY-drah), a daughter of Typhaon (TY-fah-on, Hera's monster son), infested the swamp of Lerna, not far from Nemea.

One night he knocked on my door.

I let him in. "What do you want?"

"That you stop persecuting Heracles." He sat down on my narrow bed. He propped his elbows on his knees, let his head droop, gave a heavy sigh.

" '*Persecuting* Heracles?' I thought I was obliging you with further testing of his bravery."

"Don't taunt me, Hera. We are in grave danger—"

" 'We?' I haven't thought of us as 'we' for quite a while."

"You, I, all the gods and goddesses who fought against the Titans face destruction—"

"Have the Titans broken loose from Tartarus?"

"No."

"Then who is our enemy?"

"I'll tell you, but you must swear to keep it secret—"

"Swear? *You* speak to me of swearing oaths?"

"Reprove me later. Hear me out. A race of Giants threatens us. Gaia bore them from the blood Uranus shed when Cronos cut his power from him. Her anger that we beat the Titans has been smoldering for eons. Now she has roused these Giant sons of hers to take revenge."

"What makes you think they can destroy us?"

"A certain herb that Gaia grew. I kept the sun from shining on it, and the rain from falling on it, but it would not die. It thrives. When the Giants eat this herb, they are protected against us."

"Invulnerable to us Olympians?"

"Not wholly. We can wound them, but we cannot kill them."

"Who *can*?"

"Only a mortal. One who is exceptionally brave, intelli-

When Uranus (Sky) had pressed too hard on Gaia (Earth), Gaia made a sickle, gave it to her son Cronos, and asked him to cut Uranus's powers away, which Cronos did.

gent, and strong. Oh, Hera, don't you see? It wasn't lust, it wasn't any whim of Aphrodite's that sent me to Alcmene's bed. It was strong Fate, the one called Atropos. I *had* to go to Thebes. How else but with the most exceptional of mortal women could I beget a mortal hero great enough that he might save us?" Zeus looked at me imploringly. "Hera, do you understand?"

"Yes." I put my arms around him.

Once again our marriage was renewed.

✤ The Giants lived in Phlegra, a land of fire-spewing mountains. There we went, all we immortals, accompanied by Heracles, and fought a war with them.

They were shaped like humans, but thirty times as tall, and fifty times as strong, except Porphyrion and Enceladus, their leaders, who were fifty times taller, and ninety times as strong. They used entire oak tree trunks for torches. They broke the pinnacles from mountains to throw at us, along with rocks and boulders.

Zeus, in turn, threw thunderbolts. Apollo and Artemis shot arrows by the hundreds, and never missed their mark.

Of all our deeds, this was the most astonishing: Athena, mustering immeasurable strength, lifted an island out of the sea, and hurled it at the Giant Enceladus. The island is called Sicily. Enceladus lies beneath it, trapped, crushed to a pulp, but living still. You don't believe me? Go there, and you'll see his rasping breath come up in smoke and flames from the crater in the mountain they call Etna, to this very day.

Finally all our foes lay either buried under chunks of

Atropos (AH-trop-os, "inevitable").

Phlegra (FLEG-rah), now known as Campi Flegrei, in southern Italy, is on the Bay of Naples.

Porphyrion (por-FEE-ree-on, "the purple one").

Enceladus (en-sel-AHD-us, "the one who shouts huzzahs").

islands or on Phlegra's ground, blood pouring from their wounds. Then the mortal hero Heracles ran from one foe to the next, swinging his club, dealing deadly blows to some. And those who still refused to die, he shot with arrows that he'd dipped in the Hydra's venom. In this way he fulfilled his purpose, and he saved us all.

But first he'd nobly rescued *me*, despite how much and for how long I'd plagued him. It happened in the middle of a battle. Immense Porphyrion was coming after me, eyes ablaze with lust. Between us gaped a deep, wide chasm, over which the Giant leader jumped as easily as if it were a little puddle. I willed myself away—too late. His endless arm reached out, he snatched my tunic, saw it rip, roared as loud as twenty lions in his triumph— then crashed down, felled by an arrow Heracles had shot straight through his groin.

Other heroes love to boast, but Heracles told nobody how close I'd come to being violated. He neither asked for praise nor bore me grudges for the past harms I'd done him.

Only when I thanked him from the fullness of my heart did I understand his name at last. *Cles* means "glory"; *Heracles* means "Hera's glory," which I do owe to him. For what if not my honor and my virtue constitute my glory, which, in truth, he saved?

❖ "In gratitude, make him immortal," I said to Zeus, and Zeus agreed.

We brought him to Olympus. He fell in love with Hebe, our youngest daughter; she, with him. And the wedding feast we gave them was as joyous as our own.

EPILOGUE

Author (Doris Orgel—from here on, D.O.): Would you be in my epilogue?

Reader (you): What's an epilogue?

D.O.: The place in a book to tie up loose ends and say more. Mine will have some playing, make-believe, and wishes.

You: Yes, but what does *epi* mean? And *logue*?

D.O.: *Epi* is Greek for "after," *log* is short for *logos*, or "word." I don't know what *ue* is for.

You: Why not just call it *afterword*?

D.O.: Well, the goddesses are Greek. And I love the sound of "epilogue." Words like that thrill me. But you're right. Plain words are good. Everybody understands them. Okay, let's call it *afterword*. Will you be in it? Please say yes.

You: What do I have to do?

D.O.: Get together with Athena, Aphrodite, Hera—

You: Where? How? When? Why?

D.O.: On Mount Olympus, in Zeus and Hera's feasting hall. Ask your favorite goddess, and she'll get you there. Right now. To celebrate the marriage of Hebe and Heracles.

You: Hm. How will I get back?

D.O.: The same way you came, I assume.

You: *Assume?* Aren't you sure?

D.O.: I'm never sure of anything when I first start to imagine it. Are you?

You: I guess not.

D.O.: Take a chance. What do you say? Will you be in this epi—I mean, afterword?

AFTERWORD

Your goddess gets you to Olympus.

The Hours guard the gate. They let you in and lead you to the feasting hall in Zeus and Hera's palace, built on the highest pinnacle.

Hymen, god of weddings, sings a wedding song. The Graces dance. The Muses do, too, and play their instruments. Hebe and Heracles speak their vows, give each other rings and kisses. Everyone congratulates them.

Now that Hebe's married, there's a new cupbearer: Ganymede, a Trojan boy. Zeus's eagle brought him here. He brings you a goblet, and starts pouring nectar.

Hera: Stop, Ganymede! Nectar is only for immortals!

Ganymede: Sorry. May I bring you something else?

You name a soft drink. Ganymede brings it and pours.

You look around, take in the sights. Your goddess has arranged that neither the deities' radiance nor the dazzle of the hall will hurt your eyes.

In a corner is a rounded window looking out into the sky. On a cushioned bench built along the window's curve sit Athena, Aphrodite, and Hera. They seem relaxed; they chat.

Your goddess catches sight of you and beckons. You join them.

You (*thinking, not aloud*): Are they just being friendly because it's a festive occasion?

Athena: We've made up, you see.

You (*to yourself*): Uh-oh. Can they hear what I'm thinking?

Hera: Want to know how I stopped being enemies with Aphrodite? It happened on a bloody day. The Trojan War was raging on and on. As you know, Zeus favored Troy. And I fought for the Greeks. That angered him so much, he wouldn't speak to me.

I missed his love. I wished we could be close again. But I looked haggard, battle-weary. I definitely lacked allure. How could I win my husband back?

Bath oils, lotions, perfumes didn't help. Finally, in near despair, I went to Aphrodite—

Aphrodite: I didn't make her beg or grovel. I just unclasped my golden girdle, and I told her, "Put it on." Do you remember what the poets said it can do?

You: Make whoever borrows it look wonderful?

Aphrodite: Yes.

You (*to Hera*): Then you and Zeus got back together? He loved you, and you were so happy, you stopped being mad at Aphrodite?

Hera: Right. Athena, now it's your turn. Tell what made you change your mind, or rather, change your heart.

Athena: Some things are better seen than told.

Athena touches you lightly on the forehead. A curtain opens in your mind and reveals a wooden statue—the one she carved of Pallas.

Athena: My father sent his eagle down. The eagle grasped the statue in his talons and brought it to Troy. The Trojans honored it. They named it the Palladium, and placed it in their inmost sanctuary. On the day when Troy went up in flames, Aphrodite's son, Aeneas, dashed into the sanctuary and rescued the Palladium. He guarded it all through his travels. He brought it to the city that he founded—Rome. Somewhere in that city is a sanctuary; no one knows exactly where. In that sanctuary is a niche. In that niche stands my Palladium—forever.

Athena tells this quietly, yet everybody present in the hall can hear.

Suddenly—to everybody's shock, dismay—the door bursts open. Eris, goddess of quarreling, comes in. She holds a shining golden apple in her hands.

Clio (Muse of History; *alarmed*): Not again! Didn't anybody learn a lesson? Couldn't someone have invited her?

Eris: I'm afraid the answer's no.

Clio (*appalled*): Must history repeat itself?

Eris (*smugly*): I'm afraid so. (*She comes straight over to you,* thrusts the apple in your hands.) Shall I read you the inscription, dear? It's in Greek.

You: No, thank you, I remember. It says, "To the fairest." (*You feel weird; you try in vain to hand the apple back to her.*) But, but—

Eris: No buts. This time, *you're* the judge. Go on, award it to the fairest.

You: (*thinking, definitely not aloud*): What if it makes them enemies again, and starts another war?

Athena: It won't.

You (*still not aloud*): Oh my gosh. She *can* hear what I'm thinking!

Hera, Aphrodite: Certainly. We can, too.

You: How do you do that?

Aphrodite: Nothing to it. It's like hearing what my doves say when they're cooing.

Athena: Or what my owl says when she hoots.

Hera: Or my peacock when he screeches.

You (*to yourself, very scared*): I'm in deep trouble. They hear everything I think, and I can't shut my thoughts off. Help! Somebody, stop me! I keep thinking about what I wish they'd give me, just in case they try to bribe me—

Aphrodite: Wish all you want.

Athena: Think all you want. And feast your eyes on us.

Hera: Yes, look us over, then decide.

You *(looking, thinking)*: Athena's just as I imagined. So is Hera. But Aphrodite—*(You blink; you feel a little dizzy; you have to place your feet more firmly on the bright mosaic floor.)* Not even the greatest artist could imagine what Aphrodite looks like. Aphrodite's right: She *is* perfection. There's really nothing to decide.

You offer her the golden apple.

Aphrodite *(laughs her golden laughter)*: No, thanks. I already have one, with that same inscription. Give it to one of my friends.

Athena: *I* don't want it.

Hera: *I* don't either.

Everyone watches, listens intently. In the hush you hear a repulsive sound. It's Eris gnashing her teeth. Suddenly she's in your face—

Eris: Give me back the golden apple!

She snatches it, and leaps out the window.
Everyone applauds. Music resumes. Dancing starts. There's much rejoicing in the hall.

Clio: Whew, history did *not* repeat itself.

You *(to yourself)*: Right, that's good. Even so, I'm just a little disappointed—

Aphrodite: Why? Don't forget, I heard you wishing. Look! *(A fine gold thread has loosened in her girdle. She pulls it out.)* The poets say a single thread has all the magic of the whole. Here, I give the thread to you. Treasure it. Someday it may win you what your heart desires.

Athena: I heard you wishing, too. I gave you the first part of my gift before, when I touched your forehead. It's the gift my mother, Metis, gave to me. *(She touches your forehead twice more.)* There. Now you have vision, understanding, skill.

Hera: I heard you wishing right away. When Ganymede began to pour you nectar, you wished to be immortal.

You: Yes. Who wouldn't?

Hera: And I stopped him. I made sure your wish would *not* come true. That was my gift to you.

You: Your gift was *not* making my wish come true?

Hera: That's right. It's a good gift, but the reason's too hard to explain.

Athena: Hard, but let me try: Mortality imbues each moment with a glory that we goddesses can only dream of.

You think about it.
The goddesses embrace you and invite you, "Join the feast."
When it ends, Athena brings you Pegasus, the winged horse. Aphrodite offers you her dove-drawn chariot; Hera, her chariot peacock-drawn. Any of these three will get you home.

Gorgon—Clay fragment from Syracuse, Sicily, a Greek colony, 6th century B.C. The horrible Medusa—look at her if you dare!—is giving birth to little Pegasus while being slain by Perseus (not shown).(2)

Athena flying her owl—Bronze statuette, Greek, 5th century B.C., probably found at Athens. Why did Athena keep owls as pets? Because they're wise? They're really not! It's just that the Acropolis was a favorite breeding place for owls, and many could be seen perched near or on the Parthenon, Athena's famous temple.(3)

Striding Athena— Black-figure prize amphora, Greek, Attic, late 5th century B.C. On this handsome trophy, awarded to a winner in the athletic competition held in Athena's honor, the goddess, looking confident, holds a shield with Pegasus emblazoned on it.(4)

Zeus seated—Roman copy, bronze, of a 5th-century B.C. Greek statuette. The god-king's arm is raised in welcome, perhaps to greet Athena as she comes to sit beside him.(5)

ATHENA

Athena promachos—
*Roman copy of a Greek
work from the 5th century
B.C. Athena, helmeted and
ready to go into battle for
her city.(1)*

Poseidon with dolphins
—*Red-figured neck
amphora (two-handled
container), Greek, 470-
465 B.C. The sea god,
Athena's mighty rival,
grasps a dolphin with his left
hand and the three-pronged
trident with his right.(6)*

Judgment of Paris—Pyxis
(small box or vase), white
ground, Greek, Attic, 465–
450 B.C. Paris seated, dressed
as a shepherd. Hermes (left) is
bringing Aphrodite, Athena, and
Hera (pictured on the reverse).
Zeus (right) looks on.(2)

Mirror cover—Bronze, 5th century B.C.
A lovely Aphrodite instructing Eros how to
shoot arrows from his little bow.(3)

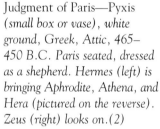

Hermes running
—Red-figured
lekythos (vase with
narrow neck),
Athenian, late 5th
century B.C. The
messenger god is
clearly in a hurry,
perhaps because he
has a date with
Aphrodite.(4)

Sleeping Eros—Bronze statuette, said to come from Rhodes,
3rd–2nd century B. C. The little love god looks peaceful and benign,
for once not causing trouble, as he does when he's awake.(5)

APHRODITE

Aphrodite with Pan
and Eros—*Marble, from
Delos, 1st century B.C.
The leering goat god starts
embracing Aphrodite. She
holds up her sandal,
possibly to strike him with
it. A mischievous Eros
looks on.(1)*

Two figures embracing—
*Fragments of a kylix
(shallow cup with tall stem).
Greek, Attic, 6th century
B.C. Clearly, it was
Aphrodite who taught this
couple how to be in love.(6)*

Rhea presenting a stone in the form of a baby to Cronos— *Red-figured pelike (wide-mouthed container for wine or water), Greek, Attic, 5th century B.C. The stone is swaddled in fine cloth, just as a baby would have been. Cronos is ready to gulp it down. Pictured here, his mouth looks small, but being a god, he surely can make it as big as he wants.(2)*

Oceanus—Bronze. Roman copy of a Greek statuette, probably 5th century B.C. This Titan is the god of the mighty river flowing all around the earth, father of all lesser rivers, and in Hera's girlhood was her foster father.(3)

Marriage of Hera and Zeus—*Fifth century B.C., found in Sicily (a Greek colony). Since there was no one more sacred or exalted than this goddess and this god, they themselves performed the world's first marriage ceremony.(4)*

Fragment from the Ludovisi Throne—*Greek, 5th century B.C. from a sculpture for the Heraeum (Hera's temple) at Argos. This marble relief shows Hera, helped by two nymphs, emerging from her bath in the river Canathus.(5)*

HERA

Giunone Regina (Queen Juno)—*Roman, 1st century B.C., probably a copy of a 5th-century B.C. Greek statue of Hera. Juno is the Roman Hera, but more imperial, a protector and upholder of the state.(1)*

Bird—*Bronze, Greek. 8th century B.C. This ancient statuette, found in Hera's temple at Argos, is not just of any bird. Its proud plume and splendid tail distinguish it as Hera's special, emblematic peacock.(6)*

SOURCES

ANCIENT:

Apollodorus, *The Library, Epitome*—Greek myth retellings from the second century B.C. Translated by Sir J.G. Frazer. Loeb Classical Library, Harvard University Press, 1921.

Callimachus, *Hymns and Epigrams*—Greek poems from the third century B.C. Translated by A.W. Mair and G.R. Mair. Loeb Classical Library, Harvard University Press, 1921.

Hesiod, *The Homeric Hymns, and Homerica*—These writings from the eighth century B.C. tell how the world began, and about the generations of gods and goddesses. Translated by H.G. Evelyn White, Loeb Classical Library, Harvard University Press, 1914.

Homer, *The Iliad*—Epic poem from the eighth century B.C. about the Trojan War. Translated by Richard Lattimore. The University of Chicago Press, 1951.

Ovid, *Metamorphoses*—Greek myths with emphasis on transformations, retold by a Roman poet of the first century B.C. Translated by Rolfe Humphries. Indiana University Press, 1955.

Virgil, *The Aenead*—The story of how the Trojan hero Aeneas founded Rome, told by a Roman poet of the first century B.C. Translated by Robert Fitzgerald, Random House, 1981.

OTHER:

Bell, Robert E., *Women of Classical Mythology: A Biographical Dictionary*. Oxford University Press, 1991.

Bowra, C. M., *The Greek Experience*. The World Publishing Company, 1957.

Bulfinch, Thomas, *Myths of Greece and Rome*. Compiled by Bryan Holme. Penguin, 1979.

Durando, Furio, *Ancient Greece: The Dawn of the Western World*. Stuart, Tabori & Chang, 1997.

Grant, Michael, and John Hazel, *Who's Who in Classical Mythology*. J.M. Dent, 1993.

Graves, Robert, *The Greek Myths*. Penguin, 1955.

Kirk, G. S., *The Nature of Greek Myths*. Penguin, 1974.

Larousse *Encyclopedia of Mythology*. Prometheus Press, 1960.

Lefkowitz, Mary, and Maureen B. Fant. *Women's Lives in Greece and Rome*. The Johns Hopkins University Press, 1982.

Rose, H. J., *A Handbook of Greek Mythology*. E.P. Dutton & Co., Inc., 1959.

Sacks, David A., *Dictionary of the Ancient Greek World*. Oxford University Press, 1995.

Seyfert, Oskar, *Dictionary of Classical Antiquities*. Meridian Books, 1956.

Switzer, Ellen, and Costas, *Greek Myths: Gods, Heroes and Monsters*. Atheneum, 1988.

Vernant, Jean-Pierre, *Mortals and Immortals*. Princeton University Press, 1991.

———. *The Origins of Greek Thought*. Cornell University Press, 1982.

Zeitlin, Froma I., and Catharine R. Simpson, *Playing the Other: Gender and Society in Classical Greek Literature*. University of Chicago Press, 1996.

PHOTO CREDITS

3. Giraudon/Art Resource, New York.

4. Scala/Art Resource, New York.

5. Erich Lessing/Art Resource, New York.

6. The Metropolitan Museum of Art, Fletcher Fund, 1935 (35.11.14).

INDEX OF PROPER NAMES